Illegal Affair
Sienna Mynx

Copyright © 2011 Sienna Mynx
All rights reserved.
ISBN: ISBN: 0615586090
ISBN-13: 978-0615586090

The Seduction

Happenstance is merely the shadow of destiny...

CHAPTER ONE

Raelynn swallowed her martini too fast. The apple-spiced vodka singed her throat and nearly came out of her nose from laughter. Cheery faces, raised voices, and glasses clinked under the dimmed lights of Foley's Bar. It was her birthday, and she knew the rules. No working, no excuses; she planned to celebrate her 30th with a bang, and damn well enjoy it. Considering most of her assignments kept her on duty round the clock and traveling 160 days out of the year it was a tall order.

What her friends didn't know was birthday or not, she'd been on a private mission of her own tonight. The plan to find the sexiest man in the bar and let go some pent-up frustration was underway. The worthy candidate had to be the complete opposite of her corporate attorney loser ex-boyfriend, Ed.

"We need more shots!" Andrea yelled, her bright-pink lips spread into a wide grin over her round face. She had auburn corded dreadlocks that were swept up neatly into a ponytail. Andrea slammed down her Patron-laced shot glass, giving the waitress a wicked a look.

"Don't let her drink another. Geez, it's Raelynn's birthday and you're acting like it's your twenty-first!" Gina cut her eyes to Raelynn's other friend, Olivia. They both shared a smirk. Everyone knew that Andrea would turn any event into her event.

"Ladies, can we join you?"

A tall, sexy ebony man with a thin mustache and lickable lips spoke up. Behind him stood three other men, equally handsome, and diverse in height and appearance. The blond locked his green eyes on her. Raelynn sipped her martini and smiled. She'd never dated a white man before. How far should this search for *Mr. Right Now* go?

"You buying?" Andrea asked.

"Ignore her. Sure, join us. Today is our friend Raelynn's birthday," said Olivia, singling out Raelynn with a manicured fingertip.

It was all she heard from the rambunctious group. In fact, everything in the room went still, including her breathing, when the wood-paneled door at the front of the bar opened. Another man entered with a swagger that could only spell trouble. Raelynn's instincts were sharp. Though he appeared dressed like the other businessmen, she could tell the suit wasn't a natural fit for him. She found him quite interesting.

"Raelynn, did you hear him? He said he wanted to buy you a drink." Olivia nudged her.

Raelynn pulled her attention from the man in a leather jacket and dark slacks just as he approached the bar. She focused on the three before her, noting their wolfish grins.

"Yeah, um, I'll have to pass. Not ready to dance yet." Raelynn returned her gaze to Foley's newest patron, and a slow, easy smile moved over her lips. "Not yet."

There has to be more to my life than this.

Several locals parted like the Red Sea to give room. Shane ignored the sideways glances from a grumbling man vacating the barstool to his left. It was because of Ian Higgins the man knew to keep his disdain in check. He reached inside his brown, weather worn leather jacket for his smokes.

To hell with it. This is as good a spot as any to cool off.

Foley's Bar was a safe haven in South Boston. You do a job and you got only a few places that could be counted on to provide cover.

Shane's gaze lifted to the mirrored wall facing the bar. He wasn't too bad off—just a few scrapes on his brow and chin. *Hell, they should see Mickey.* He didn't look away from his own reflection as the bartender pulled down bottles of private stock.

The man staring back from the glass resembled his father in every way: the same brown curl to his hair, squared brooding brow, the long sideburns and thin mustache and goatee. All of it was like the old man; including his practiced vacant stare neither friend nor foe could read.

Shane wasn't big like his father, who stood six-foot-five and weighed, at last count, close to three hundred eighty. Shane was just average in height and build. Physical appearance notwithstanding, Shane Lafferty was his father's son in every way that counted except one. Rock Lafferty was upstate doing twenty-to-life on a murder rap. Shane closed and opened his right hand, feeling the knuckles bruising and swelling. He was a lot of things, but he was no murderer. Yeah, he'd cracked Mickey's jaw. He was pretty sure he'd left him alive.

"Shane? Let's roll."

"It's hot out there now, Scotty. Sit," he mumbled, searching, patting down his pockets for his lighter and finding lint, a condom, and two sticks of gum. He wasn't wearing his favorite hoodie or jeans. Even at thirty-two, he was never caught without them. Damn tie was too much. He felt strangled by it.

In order to do the job, he and Scotty had cleaned up. He'd needed slacks, a collared shirt and tie to complete the look. The whole uptown scene would make his mother proud if she were able to put down the booze long enough to remember she had a son.

"Hell, man, we can't stay here. The cops are probably hitting each bar. We need to get back to Higgins and square up. Take the alley out. I think... I think Mickey's hurt, too. We shouldn't have left him behind."

Shane gave his cousin a silencing look, then shifted his steely gaze away. In his line of vision was a busty brunette behind the bar in a cut-off green-and-white Celtics T-shirt. He reached for the matches, drawing the attention of the waitress pouring drinks. She nodded that she'd make her way to him.

He had an eye for women. So his gaze narrowed on her tits as he took a long drag on his cigarette. She was new. It had been months since he visited Foley's, so he expected fresh faces.

If it weren't for the bank Higgins wanted them to hit, he wouldn't even bother acknowledging her. But an alibi was something he needed.

The truth was, he couldn't stand the snobby women in their suits, turning their noses up, or the uptight men who acted like his kind was invisible. The babe bartender was more his speed. Shane preferred to stay in his lane.

"Shane?"

The knot of tension at the base of Shane's neck spread evenly over his shoulders and down to his wrists. He leveled his gaze on Scotty in the long mirror above the bar. His cousin stood there panting, red in the face, his left eye closing and swelling from the smack Mickey'd given him when the teller hit the silent alarm. The bank was just eight blocks over. Shedding the workman's jumpsuits in an alley, then walking the streets in their shirt and ties was the key move to aid in their escape. But Scotty's folly and Mickey's attitude blew it all to hell.

Shane gritted his teeth. It was his fault. Decking Mickey and leaving him unconscious in a pile of steaming garbage was dumb. To hell with it! He wasn't sorry. Shane hated a bully. Kicking Scotty around was like smacking a baby—pointless and mean. Mickey got what he deserved.

"What do I care if the cops come through?" he mumbled.

There was no going back. His fate wasn't in his hands. Not since he joined Higgins payroll. This job was easy, but like always, it went down bad. They might as well let it play out.

Scotty gave an exasperated nasal whine. He shoved the loser on the barstool to Shane's left side so he could take the spot. Shane could practically hear his cousin's thoughts: *I wonder if Mickey's dead? Shane did hit him hard. Shit, we left the masks and gear in the alley with him. Can the cops* trace it back to us? I screwed up and Shane had to defend me as usual. *What will Higgins do when he finds out? Will Shane cover for me, like always?* If it weren't for his cousin's bumbling, Shane wouldn't be in this mess.

"Back off," Shane ordered. "I need to think."

Scotty did as he was told.

"What can I fix ya?" chirped the brunette with the nice rack and inflated glossy-pink lips. He hated females with fake lips. Angelina Jolie knock-offs is what he called them. This honey couldn't be any older than twenty-five. A waste.

"Guinness," Shane answered. She drew a pint. The foam rose to the top of the dark brew and the gal flipped him a sexy pout, trying to capture his attention. He met her stare but gave her nothing. She winked and moved on.

"At least the money is safe. They'll never figure out where we put it, huh, Shane? Never." Scotty gave a nervous chuckle as if he had something to do with that.

Shane inhaled the ash-flavored tobacco, allowing it to soothe him as he tuned his cousin out. He needed to think. No chance of that in a bar. Behind him, a roar of laughter could be heard over Kanye West's rhymes about the *Good Life*. His gaze slowly focused again on the mirrored surface, searching for the source. Shane honed in on a crowd gathered around a table of seated women. A group of guys were clamoring in close, while a waitress arrived with more shots. Shane exhaled a milky stream of smoke. *It's going to be a long night.*

"It's not just the cops though." Scotty started in again. "Rumor has it the Feds are onto Higgins now, which means they are on to me. Between the Feds and ATF, I got to keep a low profile. This was never your bid, Shane. I got you in this mess. You did the job to save me from Higgins. Now we got Mickey and all. I really screwed up—"

"Shut your fucking trap. You hear me?" Shane snapped through clenched teeth.

Scotty nodded obediently and signaled for a beer, shoving peanuts in his mouth to ensure his silence. Shane downed half his pint and then slammed the glass on the bar. He needed to think. He needed to calm down. He needed to find out how badly he'd hurt Mickey.

A chorus of laughter rose from the table behind him, then applause. He cast his gaze over his shoulder in search of the source. To his amusement, the ladies started chanting. *"Go Raelynn, it's yo birthday...Go Raelynn, it's yo birthday...Go Raelynn, it's yo birthday...Go! Go! Go! Go!"*

As if of one accord, the group squealed. With his curiosity piqued, Shane turned all the way around on his barstool to focus on the center of everyone's attention: a petite, dark-skinned beauty he'd definitely remember if he'd seen her before.

She tossed back the dark contents of the shot glass and then winced, choking. Shane smiled as a celebratory roar exploded through the group. One of her girlfriends rubbed her back. Two others reached over and handed her napkins to wipe what he perceived to be the sweetest pair of lips this side of the Charles River.

Now those are lips I could get with.

Shane's smirk dimmed. He'd never been with a black chick before. He wasn't opposed to it, just never considered them really. In Southie, it was Irish blood only, segregated by choice.

Sure he knew and did some deals with blacks, but they ran in their circles and he ran in his. Even so, Shane found himself unable to look away. It was true. Higgins said it all the time. He had that sixth sense built in where he could read folks. There was something buzzing about this one.

He dropped back on the bar, took another drag off his half-smoked cigarette and watched. The crowd thinned for a moment and he could see her clearly. Long bangs. High cheekbones. A sexy smile that made her eyes slant. The excitement around her, as everyone laughed and vied for her attention, was drawing looks from everyone else in the bar, not just the dressed-up schmucks around them. Then the opportunity to know more passed. Her crowd of friends swallowed her again, blocking his view from every angle.

"So um, if we're hanging here, then maybe we should call Higgins, you know? Hell, I'm worried about Mickey out there. Thanks for that, bro, sticking up for me, but I had it. Can take care of myself, ya know? Still, it's a risk, leaving him unconscious the way we did. What if he gets picked up?"

"Call Higgins. Tell him where to find Mickey. Do it and then leave."

"Sure thing... sure thing!" Scotty slammed back the last of his beer, hopped off the barstool, and hurried off.

Shane would have given the order sooner if he'd known it would get his cousin to stop bitching about it. Truth was, he loved Mickey. Mickey was the only family he had left. Why else would he risk his life this way? He had a good job at the garage. He only dealt with Higgins when he had to run something back through the Pen to his dad. But Scotty had gotten in over his head. The bank robbery was his only way out. Despite his cousin's shortcomings, Shane wasn't going to let him fall. So here he was, awaiting his fate. And fate *hated* his ass.

Shane tracked his cousin until he disappeared around a corner at the back of the bar. Foley's still had a pay phone near the bathrooms, which was a small bit of luck. Neither of them would dare use cell phones with things this hot.

Given some respite, Shane flicked ash onto the floor and studied the crowd, but his vision always shifted back to the party girl. She seemed oblivious to anyone but those inside her tight little circle. For some reason, this bothered him. He wanted her undivided attention.

"I hear there's a birthday girl in the house."

Shane pulled his gaze away to a tall blonde squeezed behind a turntable set up on the opposite end of the bar. Sporting a frizzy afro compressed by large headphones, she was dressed as if she'd just stepped out of Studio 54. *Thing must be a wig.*

"Is this true, gang?" Party Girl's crew ratted her out while she hid behind her hand. *So it's her birthday. Nice.*

"No use in hiding, birthday girl!" the blonde chuckled. "Your friends tell me you like to shake that rump to Beyoncé."

That figures. Women love Beyoncé. Every time someone puts on one of her records the babes all rush to the dance floor. As "Sweet Dreams" started pumping through the speakers, Shane's shoulders tensed. He couldn't wait to see her dance.

He wasn't disappointed. Party Girl and her crew all squealed in delight and rose at once. The jerks crowding them weren't too far behind.

The song picked up in tempo and despite her unsure footing, she put down some sexy moves. Sandwiched between two clowns, she owned them.

Shane dragged on his cigarette until it burned to the filter, putting it out. With the adrenaline from the day's events still pumping through his veins, he found himself rising from the bar. Before he could wrap his head around what he was doing, he'd made his way through the maze of pub tables and stepped through the crowd of partiers to stand directly in front of her.

Of course she didn't notice him right away, but the clowns did. None of them stepped back. It took a moment for her to turn and realize he was there for her. Her dance moves slowed as she stared up at him. He smirked, arching his brow. Not a word passed between them, but she knew. It was clear what he wanted.

The birthday girl smiled. Moving to the beat, she slipped sideways between two of the clowns and started dancing close, closer, dropping her arm on his shoulder. She wound her hips up against him, her eyes never leaving his. Bozo and Bubbles scuttled away. Any man watching could see this dance was only between him and her.

Party Girl lifted her arm to his neck and closed her eyes, continuing to sway and swing her hips in that tasty way. Shane wasn't a dancer, but he was heavily considering lessons, just for her. The birthday girl didn't find it odd that he didn't move under her instruction. He guessed those Jaegers must've had her feeling him, too.

Her giggling girlfriends took notice. The one with the red locks and large cherry lips clapped and cheered Party Girl's name from the sidelines. It appeared she was called Raelynn. He repeated it over and over as her breasts rubbed to erect points against his chest.

Someone snapped a picture. He barely noticed. How could he with the way she moved? Beyoncé could take a dance lesson or two from Miss Raelynn. His temptress turned on him, putting her backside to his groin, sliding up and down, rolling her ass, snug in its tight mini, all over him. This, he was feeling. His arm slipped around her waist. She smelled expensive. Probably worked in one of the offices downtown. She was fine too, every curve soft and supple. What was a man to do? As the song ended and she turned in his arms, he put both of his around her to keep her there and let her know *this* was far from over.

"Happy birthday, Raelynn," he said.

She dropped her head back, her lips curling up in a sly smile. "How'd you know my name?"

"Made it my business to," he said.

"And how'd you know it was my birthday?" she asked.

"Lucky guess."

"So you just lucky, huh?"

"I am right now."

She chuckled, a soft peal of laughter that blended with the slow groove now playing. He took the liberty to feel her and she didn't shy away from his touch. Now the night had purpose. Maybe fate didn't hate his ass. The birthday girl was hitting all the right spots in his arms. Even though he'd first taken her for some easy broad that dated men whose asses he'd probably kicked in grade school, now he could see she was much more than that. There was a light of awareness in her eyes and a toughness he didn't pick up on in many women. There was something... something he couldn't quite put a name to.

"You're hurt?" she asked, reaching to touch the bruise over his eye. "How'd that happen, Mr. Lucky?"

Shane had completely forgotten it, giving no thought to how bad it must appear. It definitely knocked off his cool points. He smiled, trying to cover. "I tripped, baby, trying to get over here next to you."

Raelynn's thin eyebrows dropped. Under curled lashes, her eyes seemed to darken to liquid pools of chocolate. A brief shiver went through him. There was something authoritative about her stare, and an ageless *awareness*, one he'd never quite appreciated before in a woman. In a flash, the probing stare softened, but still, the hairs at the nape of his neck stood on end. Something wasn't quite right with this one. What was he missing?

"Smooth, I like it," she said softly.

She wasn't shy either. When he ran his hand down her backside, she didn't seem fazed. Yes, she owned him, and it was damn sexy.

Shane Lafferty knew to always play it safe and to keep his head when it came to people he didn't know, especially women. He kept his guard up on all things. But there was something about her, this dance and her beauty. Something he couldn't quite turn away.

She shifted against him. He felt her readiness to bolt, back away.

He dismissed the warning bells ringing in his head and calmed his nerves. He was just jumpy, and rightfully so. He needed to chill. Why not do that in her arms? It was the best place to be at the moment.

"Your name?" she asked, continuing to groove to the music and causing his hips to sway, if only to enjoy the tasty waves of her lower body against his. He had to beat back his erection with a mental stick.

"Shane, but most call me Lafferty."

"Lafferty. I like that. A true Irish boy's name."

"I haven't been a boy for a very long time, sweetheart."

Again she laughed, it sounded more like a sweet chuckle that made her breast jiggle against him. She was a foot shorter than he, but her curves pressed against him nicely in all the right places.

"Lafferty?"

"Yes?"

"The music stopped," she said sheepishly.

He hadn't realized. He was so fixated on her, he barely heard the DJ announce her break or see the others leave the small dance floor. Reluctantly, he let Raelynn go. "Your fault. You distracted me."

She pressed her lips together as if to stifle a smile. Was she laughing at him? It felt like it.

"Want to join me and my friends?"

Shane looked back at the table. It wasn't his scene. A roughneck like him amongst all these suits just didn't look like a good fit. "I'll let you get back to your friends. Happy birthday, love," he said, squeezing her hand. "Thanks for the dance."

He caught a light of disappointment in her eyes, but it was brief. She shrugged as if it were his loss and strutted away. He was right about her ass. It was nice. Checking his watch, he noted the time. Only half an hour had passed. It was going to be a long night. Instead of the bar, he decided to hole up in one of the booths. Plus, from there he could see her clearly. Lust or not, she wasn't someone he was quite ready to shake.

"Cousin." Scotty flopped down. "I spoke to Big Al and he said they'd bring Mickey in. The boss wants to see you in the morning. First thing. I swear, man, if we get out of this, I'm done. No more. I can't thank you enough for saving my ass."

Shane reached in his pocket for his cigarettes and then remembered he'd left the matches on the bar. Spotting a waitress, he lifted his arm. "Sweetheart, bring me a pitcha' of Harp, will you?" When she nodded and walked away with her tray raised above her head, he relaxed and slumped back.

"You better go straight. Clean. I'm tired of saving your ass. Look at my old man. He'll never be free of those prison walls. You want that? What we did today should be the end of it. Thankfully, no one got hurt."

"Mickey..."

Shane motioned with his hand to shut him up. "Like I said, no one got hurt. It ends. Tonight."

Scotty gave a skittish laugh. "I can leave you the Chevy. Not comfortable driving it since...well, you know. I called Sheila. She's gonna pick me up from Andrew Station. Think I'll chill at her place and meet you at Higgins in the morning. That cool?"

"Fine, go." Scotty blinked, a little unsure of the offering. Shane continued, "I mean it. I'll catch up with you in the morning and I'll bring in the money. Got it covered."

Scotty put the car keys on the table and eased out of the booth. Shane kept his eyes trained on the birthday girl and her party. He barely noticed as Scotty beat it for the door.

Two beers later and several passing glances between him and her from across the bar, he tired of the game and gave up on the idea of pursuing it further. What was the point? Maybe that spark of familiarity was all in his head. He wasn't a bad-looking guy. He knew it. But he definitely considered himself the polar opposite of what this one was looking for. So when she rose with her friends, he let her go. It seemed it was for the best, because she never looked back.

Shane had one more beer for the road, which he polished off in minutes and then made his way to the door. Wasted and wanted, he needed to lay low until morning. Exiting the bar, he hit the sidewalk and kept going.

CHAPTER TWO

Downtown Boston cloaked in the night held an eerie quiet. There was no traffic at this late hour. Nothing out of the ordinary moved, except for the chill gusts of wind ruffling his hair. Burying his hands deep in his pants pockets, he groaned over the fact he'd chosen his dusty leather jacket over his warm coat that he left in the car. Lost in his thoughts, if he hadn't looked up when he passed the alley, he would have missed it, missed her.

Raelynn was dressed in a warm-looking long, grey cashmere coat, her hair crowned with fallen snow as she paced the side of her car. Her cell phone was to her ear, but she wasn't talking. Shane watched her a beat, then turned down the alley. She saw him half way through his approach and ended her call. "Lafferty?"

"Trouble sweetheart?"

Frustrated, she pointed to the flat tire.

"Got a spare?" he asked, eyeing the damage.

"You going to change it in the snow? Out here in the cold?

Where's your coat? That leather jacket isn't enough, is it?"

He blew out a frosty breath and looked around, then shrugged off her question. "Where's your friends?"

"They left. I just realized it was like that when I tried to drive off, so I pulled off the road down into here. Not too smart, huh?" She smiled.

"No. A pretty girl like you should be more careful. There are shady characters out here."

I'm one of them.

She feigned being stunned and stood there staring. He realized she didn't have that shy reflex most women had around him. She met his stare dead on, each and every time.

"So you got a spare?"

"Don't know. Probably."

"Pop the trunk. Let's see."

"Why?"

Shane paused. "I'll be your lucky charm tonight and get you out of here."

It was her turn to pause, as if she were trying to decide on something. The cold was bitter. He was freezing his nuts off. The alley was dank with re-freezing slush. He thought he caught the scurry of something in the shadows near the wall. When he looked around, red beady eyes glared back at him through the darkness. This was ridiculous. Why was she giving him a hard time? What was her deal? Did she want help or not?

"How about a ride, instead?"

Now it was his turn to be surprised. "You asking me for a ride?"

"That a problem?"

"What about the call you made?"

"What about it?" she shot back.

"I dunno," he stumbled. "I'm sure your friends will come through, especially if you let them know."

"So you're turning me down?"

She gave him a sweet pout. Confused and a little bemused, Shane scratched the back of his head trying to tell if she was flirting or jerking him around.

"So?"

"Sure, I can swing it. Give you one. A ride."

"I'm sure you can," she said, looking somewhere between his waist and knees. Shane balled his fists, completely up for the challenge. She was teasing him. He liked it.

"You think you can handle it, sweetheart?"

Again, she arched a well-plucked brow. "I just turned thirty, so I think that makes me a big girl."

Shane undressed her with his eyes. "Wow, the lady isn't just beautiful, but she knows what she likes. I'm parked around back." Quickly he assessed the situation. "What about your car?"

"Who says it's my car?"

"I thought..."

"Belongs to the people I work for. They can pick it up for me," she responded with another smile.

"Then consider me your knight in shining armor."

"So chivalry isn't dead. Cute."

She winked, walked off. He watched her go and shook his head.

This night was definitely one for the record books. First it was the job that could cost him his freedom and now he faced a beautiful woman above his station in life, who apparently wanted him without questions. And he was no fool. This babe knew what she was doing. She had marked him as hers. But why? He was kind of looking forward to where it would lead.

If he hadn't come along when he did, she was going to be stuck waiting on a tow. There was no point in calling her girls. She'd put Andrea in a cab, and she was sure Olivia and Gina were on the expressway by now. Besides, it was her birthday. She'd chosen him to be her present.

He was kind of rugged. Definitely not her type. Her job had turned her stomach to urban bad boys. Maybe she was wrong about him. He was quite chivalrous, almost respectful, and a little shy, with that crooked grin of his. She was tired of lonely nights. Besides, Raelynn knew how to handle herself. Shane Lafferty was indeed luckier than he knew. He was going to be hers.

"So, it's your birthday," he stated rather than asked, not sure what else to say. He figured it as good a place to start as any. Her smoky brown eyes slipped over to him, then away. Shane smiled. "You have a good one?"

"Yeah, it was fun. My girls can be a bit wild when the liquor pours. We haven't partied like that since... before I went... well, before. Let's just say this birthday was different." She gave him a look. "Hopefully, it's not over yet."

"Yeah?"

"Definitely."

Taking the next turn, Shane asked, "Where you from, Raelynn?"

"Where you from?" she shot back again with smugness. Before he could answer, she pointed ahead. "There. My brownstone is just past the next corner."

Shane made the turn at the light.

"Park under the street light."

She opened her purse and retrieved her keys. As he set the brake, his stomach grew tight with nervous energy. This babe was definitely of a different kind. Maybe he should offer to do it right and take her to dinner. Hell, a show. He didn't know. It just felt weird if they just ended up in her bed.

"What are you waiting for? An engraved invitation?"

The question rattled in his skull. He wasn't sure she'd asked it. "You want me to come inside?"

"My birthday and I'm thinking I don't want it to end." She looked him over. "Not yet."

He dropped his hand on the back of headrest, eyeing the separation at the folds of her coat, which showed just a hint of cleavage. His gaze lingered before moving back up to capture her sexy, thickly-lashed eyes. "You don't know me."

"Sure I do. You're Shane Lafferty, the first guy all night to wish me happy birthday and not mean it."

"How's that?"

"You didn't mean it, did you? Just a good opener to get a lap dance from me while standing up."

He laughed. "Yeah, I guess."

She smiled.

Shane was at a sudden loss for words. He stared at her under the cover of darkness in his car, trying to decide. Then she decided for him. Opening her door, she got out and walked away.

"Shit!" Shane cursed, hurrying to do the same. He met her at her door just as she unlocked it, and followed her inside.

His brown beauty, elusive and mysterious most of the night, tossed the key into a candy dish and started up the stairs. Shane locked the door, immediately assessing the setup. Normally, he could tell a lot about a person by their home, that reading-people thing again. But here, he couldn't tell anything. She had empty beige walls and uncomfortable-looking furniture. However, he did notice that the place was pretty dark, which could mean they were alone.

Intrigued, Shane took his time climbing the stairs, using her sexy fragrance to guide him. Several rooms flanked the second-floor landing, but there was only one door open, light spilling out onto the wood floor. Shane ran his hand down the wall as he approached. Just shy of the threshold, he stopped and watched her.

Raelynn was inside with her back to him, dropping her purse in a chair, shedding her coat. Her legs, smooth and sexy, extended from a skirt that was fitting just right. She tossed her long bangs and flashed him that killer smile. "You going to stand there and watch or come in?"

"What's the deal with you?" he asked. "It's been my experience that when something is too good to be true, it definitely is. You don't strike me as the kind of girl that picks up strange men in bars."

Raelynn shrugged off the question. "Shane Lafferty, you're a tough guy, right? I wouldn't take you as someone to play it safe. Don't start now by questioning a gift."

Shane walked in. The physical attraction was so binding he had no choice. "You stay here?"

"Why?"

He eyed the room, remembering the emptiness downstairs. It looked carefully decorated, nothing personal. He'd done enough jobs in his past life working for the Higgins to know the difference between a home and just a house. "Your place doesn't look lived in."

"If you must know, I'm house-sitting. Enough with the questions. Are you staying or not? It's my birthday and all. Or does that matter?"

He gave her a wolfish grin. "Be careful about that birthday wish, sweetheart. I can deliver." He touched her face, then cupped her neck from behind and pulled her close, needing to silence her sass.

Her plush, supple lips parted for him. She offered her tongue immediately, teasingly. Eyes closed, her lashes spread over her high cheekbones. He brought her up against him, holding her and deepening the kiss, not closing his eyes even for a second. He wanted to see her. Dark hair cascaded down her shoulders and back. She was fated to be his. This moment was meant to be. His luck was changing.

Raelynn placed her hands between them, against his chest, kissing him as he walked her back to the bed. She helped him shed his leather jacket, remove his tie, and then unbutton his shirt. He did the same, getting her out of her shirt, popping buttons he cared little about; he peeled off her snug-fitted skirt and tiny white lace panties.

One good look and desire for her consumed him, burning him bad from within. They tumbled to the bed, and he moistened his lips, staring at her pussy with lust. He touched her inner thighs as she parted them for him to get a better look. Then he lightly caressed the neatly shaved hairs covering the top of her sex.

"Beautiful. Damn, you're so sexy."

"Mmmm," she moaned.

Shane stroked her with his middle finger, relishing her slick, satiny wetness. His eyes locked on hers. Disappointingly, her bra remained. He wished he had removed it, too. She gave a sultry growl in response to his finger-play, arching off the bed. He wanted nothing more than to pull down his pants, get in her, and thrust the ache in his cock deeply into the warm tightness he felt closing down on his fingers. Imagining how good it would be almost caused him to burst. But he forced himself to wait and to delay his own pleasure, because this was about far more than his own ecstasy.

"What you waiting for, lover?" she teased.

Shane smirked. He had to get out of his head. Go with the flow. It was, after all, her birthday. But, really, who was she? All he knew at the moment was Raelynn. He didn't even know her last name. He lowered his head, deciding it didn't matter, as he moved his tongue over her stomach. Then he returned to her navel to dip it in, inserting another finger into the wetness below. She gasped, sweetly. Beads of sweat formed over his forehead from the restraint he summoned, barely, at the sound of her soft weep for more. He wanted all of her. She was just that uniquely beautiful and enticing.

He lapped at her with the full width of his tongue. She kicked her feet, bouncing her ass on the mattress wildly when he abandoned the licks for long sucks of her clit. The torture became too much: she sat up with his head buried between her legs, trying to escape. He refused her any release. To his delight, she accepted his offering, going weak.

Raelynn removed her bra as his reward. He lifted from the pursuit of her sweet juices to see the dark swell of her fully erect nipples. Insane with lust, he placed his hand to her stomach and pushed her back down, dipping his tongue in one last time to taste her sweetness before easing up to run it over her nipple.

Her hands slid between them and undid his pants, lowering the zipper. He sucked her nipple, squeezing the other breast with his free hand and then rubbing his open palm over her mound, all the while fingering her deeply. She tensed and trembled beneath him. Then her hand eased inside his pants and gripped his cock, breaking his will. He released her nipple and closed his eyes to her.

She gave long strokes to his dick until his balls grew tight and the urge to explode was close-so-close, almost there. She was good, damn good. And that was just her hand. He leaned forward and whispered against her ear. "You sure about this, sweetheart? You had plenty to drink."

She flicked her tongue at his ear and then giggled. "I'm good."

"Good, then keep it tight for me. Don't come until we're ready. I want," he breathed deeply, "to join you."

Their eyes met, with her staring sexily under a veil of lashes. He moved off her, removing his pants, dropping them and his underwear but not before fumbling after the condom he'd found earlier. She rose up on the bed, positioning herself and watching.

He knew that look. She was checking to see if the myth was true. He wondered what black women thought of white boys and if they believed that bullshit. Her smile revealed her approval—myth shattered. He rolled the condom over his painfully swollen shaft and returned to her, stopping to run his tongue over her lower leg, knee, thigh, and the stripe of hair shaved low over her pussy. Then the seduction included her navel, her stomach and her breast before he kissed her pert nipple. He positioned himself back between her legs. He rubbed his thickness over her, wet, sweet, and warm, feeling it all through his condom.

Raelynn was ready. This would be good. He lowered his body to hers and kissed her lips. She sighed against his mouth, her legs parting wider and her hips rolling to entice him to take the plunge. One look into her soft brown eyes and the fierce light of defiance there proved she was ready for the ride. Then she gasped, her mouth forming a small 'O' as he thrust into her.

She tensed as he gripped her hips and pinned her for inch-by-inch penetration. Shane drew in a stiff breath at the punch of pleasure that hit him square in the chest as he sank balls deep. Shocked by the instant rush, he drew back and then thrust into her again and again and again with increasing roughness. Groaning aloud, he held her hips tight, riding her hard until their bodies were slick with sweat.

Her dark hair twisted and tangled around her shoulders. Every time he thrust into her, her breasts bounced softly against his chest. And instead of slowing down his strikes by tightening her muscles, she instead gripped his hips and threw hers upward to get him to go harder, faster, and that was second to the look in her eyes, pulling him, pushing him to take her further. It was screwing with his head big-time. Her cries eclipsed his as he drew inward, focusing on the inevitable, as they fell into a final explosive climax. It was the first time in his life he saw stars bursting before him during an orgasm. He dropped on her, exhausted. She hugged him as he shook out the last of his seed, stroking his ass through it. Then he slipped away, safe in the softest place on earth.

It must have been the beers. Why else would he black out after sex? Shane opened his eyes and blinked through the blinding headache that pierced his temples. He looked over to see his beauty had rolled over to her side. Suddenly, all of it, including the delicious feeling of her body and sex came rushing back. He lifted the blanket to look at her backside. She was real. It went down just as he remembered it, with a birthday girl named Raelynn. He wanted to learn everything about her. Hearing the buzz of his phone from his pant pocket, he threw back the sheet and carefully left the bed, trying not to wake her. He checked the missed calls. It was Higgins, which was a surprise. He never used his cell phone after a job. He needed to check in.

Then...

His gaze turned to sleeping beauty. He remembered. There was a more important priority of finding out why and how someone like Raelynn came into his life. Smirking, he walked toward the bed, his dick thickening against his thigh. Accidentally, he stepped on her purse. The buckle cut into the bottom of his foot. He looked down to pick it up and a billfold fell out. At first he thought it was a man's wallet. Then, suddenly, he knew it wasn't. It was as if the world slowed to a stop. Shane knelt to the carpet and picked it up, flipping it open. A badge.

In his hand was a badge. A Federal badge that belonged to Agent Raelynn Traylor 09343.

"Shit."

"Mmmm..." she moaned, turning over.

He looked at her, shocked. "You're a FED?"

She squinted at him from under her long, disheveled bangs. "What are you doing with that?" she yawned.

"Answer me. Are you a Fed?"

Raelynn sat up and smiled. "Yes. Now answer me. Why do you care?"

"Didn't say I did," Shane snapped. He hadn't meant to. Fuck. He was screwed. How the hell did he end up in the bed of a federal fucking agent? Did she know who he was? Under the gauzy silver beams of moonlight slipping in through the blinds, she stared at him, beautiful and deceptively quiet. What the hell was he to do now?

"Shane, come here." "Ah, sweetheart. I think I should go."

"Do you?" she asked softly. Not a hint of surprise in her voice. Fuck! She knew who he was. She had to know. Shane turned and snatched up his boxers. He found his pants and quickly yanked them on. Raelynn reclined into the pillows, watching him. "This was great, sweetheart. You were great, but um, I gotta head out. You know? I—um, nothing personal."

"Shane, wait."

This was it. She would give the signal and a team of armed men would flood the room. Jail. He figured one day he'd end up there. His old man predicted it. But he never figured his slip to be this. Not this.

Shane stood at the side of the bed with his shirt in his hand. He waited with stilled breath as she slipped from the covers. How could he breathe with her walking toward him, with every beautiful inch of her body on display?

"I had a good time. It doesn't have to end so soon." she chuckled. She stared up at him, obviously weighing her words. "Look, I know you're no boy scout."

"What the hell does that mean?" He stumbled back.

"It means what it means."

She crossed her arms over her breasts. He tried not to look at her pussy or acknowledge the erection forming from her being so close.

"You think I'm some kind of thug?"

She arched her brow. "I think things were good and can still be good. Then we can go our separate ways. Unless my job makes you nervous? Is that it, Shane? Do I make you nervous?"

He pulled on his shirt. She was toying with him. Challenging him. Again he had the uneasy feeling that his freedom hung in the balance and that she knew *who* he was. "Like I said, it was good. Um, happy birthday."

Those were the final words he said before he broke for the door, hurried down the stairs, and out into the street. It wasn't until he was on the sidewalk he dared a look back. She watched him from the window with the blinds pulled aside. He could see those deep brown eyes, the ones he was sure would follow him into a sleepless night. A sly smile formed on her lips before she let the blinds go and slipped away.

"Fuck. Fuck. Fuck!" he cursed. He was in the car and racing down the street before he could finally process a thought. And it was a single thought. *Did she make me?*

"You look like hell."

"Good morning to you, too," Raelynn said, easing behind her desk. The cup of coffee was her second. Already she was thinking she'd need a third.

"Party hard, did ya?"

Andy O'Brien, her partner, had missed the party but apparently had heard all about it. When he smiled, his blue eyes danced. A ginger with a face dotted with freckles, she'd been paired with him since the day she'd been assigned to the Boston field office. And they still were relegated to desk duty and paperwork. What the agency referred to as fieldwork only came after their superiors assigned every other agent above their pay grade. It was just another reason she felt the itch to rebel.

"I partied, but party over. So, give me some quiet while I wake up." She yawned.

"Sure thing, but Garrett is asking for you."

"Huh?" Raelynn sat upright. She double-blinked. The SAC was looking for her? "What did you say?"

"He came by twice. Guess you better wake up. Here he comes."

Raelynn nearly spilled the steamy coffee in her lap. She cursed under her breath, setting the mug on the desk as Garrett strode up.

"Agent Traylor, need you to come with me."

"Yes, sir." She rose and hurried behind him. Immediately, flashes of her partying last night and the cutie she'd seduced without a second thought came to mind. Was she being watched? Had she broken protocol? Why would Garrett want to speak to her without Andy? This couldn't be good.

"Have a seat, Traylor," he ordered, walking around his desk.

Raelynn wanted to remain standing, but she did as she was told.

"I'm pulling you off the Muhammad case. We need you on something more pressing."

"Sir? My own assignment?"

Garrett leveled his cool, gray eyes on her. "Is that a problem?"

"No, sir. I—"

"Good. The offender is Ian Higgins. We believe he's responsible for a spree of bank robberies on the south side." He picked up a folder and passed it over to Raelynn. "These are the jackets on his crew. We want Higgins. He's our target. Somehow, we need to find a weak link in his organization. Something we can use. Read the file. Give me an outline by the end of the day. "

Raelynn opened the file. She thumbed through the mug shots, surveillance photos. "Yes, sir. Will I be working with a team?"

"We got ATF involved and Director Greaves is commanding the internal task force. Consider it an evaluation. Show us what you can do."

Raelynn wanted to grin but knew not to. She kept her face stoic, going through the images. "I think I—"

Her voice caught. Her hand froze on the bottom image. The camera lens had captured a beat-up car and a tall, built guy with a clover tattoo on his neck and a mean-looking swagger. It was indeed the car she'd rode in. She knew that tattoo. She knew the guy. It was Shane Lafferty.

"Problem, Traylor?"

"Uh... huh? No, um, sir, no. No problem."

"Then get to it."

Raelynn swallowed. "Yes, sir. Right away sir," she mumbled, rising and bolting for the door. Her heart hammered in her chest. She avoided her desk, where she was sure Andy waited with a million questions. Instead, she beat a hasty retreat to the bathroom. It wasn't until she was alone in a stall that she opened the file with shaking hands and checked the image again. It was Shane. There was no mistaking him.

"Sweet Jesus. What the hell have I done?"

Temptation
Volume II

CHAPTER THREE

Once known as Dorchester's Neck, the Irish born residents of South Boston fondly referred to their neighborhoods as Southie. Shane Lafferty just called the place home. Now thanks to gentrification demolishing tradition and all that was familiar, Southie had quickly transformed into a wasteland of overpriced condos and swank eateries he wouldn't dine in if President Obama himself paid the tab. The Mayor's dickhead plan to remake everything north of First Street, had backing from one of the most powerful men in Boston. Ian Higgins.

Ole Danny Boy was a popular restaurant many frequented. Higgins, the owner, had several offices above it. Shane entered through the back door, which was expected. The eyes of others followed him as he walked through the kitchen where several chefs cooked over open flames for hungry patrons, and waiters rushed in and out with plates. In both of Shane's clenched hands were zipped duffle bags that weighed at best count twenty pounds each. Given the weight he knew they contained more money than he'd ever scored on any job. His father would be so proud.

"You're late Shaney," Big Al said from the top of the stairs with his arms crossed over the expanse of his wide chest. Shane lifted his gaze. He nodded gloomily. Al was several inches taller with a shaved meaty head, and a beard that covered half his face. Even in the dim lighting of the breezeway, Higgins's top enforcer's eyes shone with mockery. Shane gritted his teeth and started to climb the stairs. Al knew his father. Most men in Southie that worked for Higgins knew his father. But Al, like the old man, was the only one to refer to him as Shaney. He hated the tag.

"Is he in?"

"Oh he's in. And he's waiting." Al turned and Shane followed, but soon was blocked short of walking inside the open door. Shane bit down hard on the inside of his jaw to keep from yelling at Al to step away. Al's lips twisted into a cynical smile. "You smell like shit."

Shane lifted the bag in his left hand. It reeked from the dumpster he dug it out of. Al ignored the reference continuing to give him a once over, possibly to sniff out weakness, deceit, fear. Shane had no fight left in him. He was still spooked after a night of reckless sex with a federal agent. Raelynn, the feel of her, the sound of her soft whimpers when his cock was buried deep, and her laughter when they parted, all of it haunted him. He even thought he caught a whiff of her perfume before he went dumpster diving behind Tao's Cleaners. He was almost certain he spotted her when he sat at a traffic light waiting for fate to make it change. Raelynn, the Federal Agent with a body of a Goddess, had done him in.

"So that's it?" Al's voice boomed. He remained frozen,

immovable before the door.

"Nah, it's my laundry." Shane drawled.

Al chuckled, his Adam's apple bobbed in his thick neck.

"C'mon in Shaney," he said then stepped aside.

Shane gripped the bags tighter. The strong scent of tobacco wafted through the filtered air of the loft office. The strikingly strong aroma mixed with the spice of expensive cologne and whiskey. That was the smell of men of importance. At least that's it what he thought when he'd sat on his father's knee as a kid while he handled business for Ian Higgins.

He cast his gaze to the left and saw his cousin seated on the sofa. Next to him was Mickey. Their eyes met. Shane had to be mindful of his own strength. The side of Mickey's face from brow to cheek was red, purple with swelling. Shane let his gaze shift back to Scotty. His cousin had a Red Sox cap pulled low on his head. Something was off by his demeanor. The delivery of this money would set Scotty free. That was the deal he made. One job, one time, and they both were out of this life for good. Shane could get in the ring again, earn the boxing title he let slip from his grasp and not fuck it up with these cursed allegiances that never caused him anything but harm. He and Scotty would do something with their lives. That was the plan.

A soft click was heard from the right. Shane's head turned. He watched a white golf ball roll over the dark hardwood floors and into a stationary golf cup. Higgins looked up from his putting lean with his hands still firmly placed on the grip of the club. "Put my money down," he said.

Shane nodded and placed the money bags on the office desk.

He stepped back an appropriate distance, remaining silent as was expected when in Higgins's presence. But being humble wasn't in Shane's DNA, so his jaw twitched from the restraint of trying to remain quiet.

"The delay?" Higgins asked as he smoothly hit another ball into the cup, and one of his men took the bank loot out of the office to have the money counted.

"I had to be sure things were cool," said Shane.

"Cool? Interesting. You're concerned with things being cool. From what I hear, being cool wasn't in the plans yesterday. Am I right Mickey?" Higgins stood upright.

"Yes boss. Things got out of hand." Mickey said. Shane didn't bother to acknowledge what was inferred. No need in explaining the bruising on Mickey's face. He meant to do it. He'd do it again if Mickey so much as breathed his way. Ian Higgins smirked.

Though powerful, and respected, he wasn't a handsome man. He was about five ten, with reddish brown hair. A scar traveled from his left ear to the corner of his mouth. Plastic surgery had almost smoothed the grotesqueness of it away, except when he smiled. Ian Higgins had the devil's smile. He had a thin face, with sunken jaws and beady eyes that seemed to never blink. Looking into his clear grey irises was always an uncomfortable experience. They impaled, and almost always seemed to glisten with cold malevolence.

Dressed in dark slacks and a loose fitted blue shirt, he employed a very nonchalant manner when he spoke. "So Scotty called. Imagine my surprise when I'm told we need to pick up Mickey, yet no one tells me where my money is. I'm disappointed Shane. I called you personally, and you didn't answer. I find that rude."

"Things got complicated. I didn't mean to put you off. I was trying to work things out. The streets were swarming with cops after the robbery. We had to keep a low profile." Shane said through clenched teeth. *Things got complicated alright. Pussy always complicates things when you check your common sense at the door.* His mind flashed to the call he received from Raelynn's bed, and again his loins ached for her in remembrance. "I, um, I wanted to make sure I had my hands on your property before I returned your call. I know you prefer results not excuses."

Higgins's brows lowered and his mouth took on an unpleasant twist. He leveled the golf club at Shane. "Are you fucking with me?"

"No."

A long pause, then nothing. No one in the room dared breathe.

Higgins's mouth pulled into a sour grin. "That's why I like you Lafferty. You and I understand each other, just like me and your old man once did."

Shane exhaled the breath he'd been holding. He needed to get to the ring. Cass would be furious if he arrived late for his sparring match.

"So um, things settled then? Scotty and I…"

"Aren't done."

"I need to go," Shane said, standing his ground. Ian's left brow shot upward at his refusal. "I'm still in training." He clarified.

"Yes. The re-match of the year. Your return to the ring is causing a little buzz. Not many have forgotten your last bout with KB.

Some think you threw that fight, you and I know better. Don't we? Now you want another shot at your belt. Hmm. I have my concerns."

"Concerns?"

"I hear you decided Cass O'Leary should manage you? And after the generous offer I made?"

"He's always been my manager. Always will be." Shane said.

Ian's smile spread wider. "Have I not been good to you? When your old man got that raw deal and Margene had issues with raising you, was I not there? And that accident that could have sent you and your mother to jail, who took care of that? How do you repay me? You throw the towel in, give up and disappear on us. Now you want your title back, but you don't want me? I'm hurt."

Shane nearly laughed in his face. Good to him? He just had him rob a bank under the threat of killing his cousin over gambling debts. Why his father never saw Ian for the scumbag slug he was, he had no clue. As for the guilt over the car accident that kept him from the ring, he never asked Higgins for his help or the cover up. Shane looked to his cousin then back to Higgins. Was this a set up? Did he have him rob the bank to put him back under his control? Did Scotty even have a debt with this madman?

Ian accepted his silence as agreement. "Maybe we should discuss loyalty. We're family after all. Shane is back home, boys, it's time we celebrate his return. This pleases me. My company will be handling the promoting and bookings for this match, as well as the management of all the fighters at Gladiators."

"With all due respect. We're done. Scotty and I delivered. I only signed on to um, see this through, but I…"

"Thank you for your respect Shane. It's appreciated, but things aren't settled. You were right, your job yesterday got complicated. You left a scent that cost me money and time to clean up. Now, sit down. I'll explain to you what you can do to make things up to me."

Shane looked over to Scotty who dropped his head. Mickey however sneered with smug satisfaction. With no other choice he sat and listened, but he'd be damned if any man, especially Ian Higgins, determined his fate.

**

Raelynn had heard enough. Two hours of debriefing and she felt sick with rage. Watching the Director Elliot Greaves, and a new female Director from the ATF by the name of Melissa Harvey, she tried to maintain focus. But how could she? Beyond reason, her gaze constantly returned to the wall of photos. Six men were tacked on the glossy surface in the shape of the pyramid. These men were labeled as soldiers. Simply put they were thieves. Shane Lafferty's photo was at the bottom left, a mug shot image that revealed little but his disdain for the law.

My daddy would be so proud.

Raelynn looked away. She shifted in her seat recalling her game. Seducing Shane into her bed was strictly based on misguided rebellion. Riding his cock until her back gave out was also thanks to her stale love life after the split from her deadbeat ex-boyfriend. Letting Shane Lafferty take over her body until they both lay exhausted, and sticky with sweat, was lust pure and simple. No crime here. Though she admitted to feeling a bit more when she reached for him and inhaled the sheets in the morning just to get another whiff of his clean male scent. Oh yes, she remembered everything about his touch. Dammit how stupid! She knew better.

"Any questions?" Melissa Harvey walked the line of seated agents in her sensible shoes and dark blue pantsuit. The ATF Director's hair was jet black like her penetrating eyes. It cascaded around her face framing her delicate features. But she spoke with authority and her rigid stance commanded respect. This is what Raelynn aspired to be: fierce, committed, driven and respected. Several times her own beauty distracted the men she was partnered with. That's why she never crossed the line at work. Never.

So why did you last night?

Raelynn's hand shot up, when no one raised theirs. Melissa Harvey noticed immediately and nodded her way. She cleared her throat. "You said that the robberies are linked to those men?" she pointed the pen in her hand to the gang in which her night lover was prominently a member of. "Are they under surveillance?"

Raelynn held her breath. This was the question that had been slamming against her chest each and every passing minute. She had to know the truth. Did the Director know about what she did with Shane? Is that why her Section Chief selected her for this assignment? How bad was she in this mess?

"No." Melissa answered for Director Greaves. "We had no link between the robberies and Ian Higgins's organization until yesterday."

"An informant?" Raelynn asked.

Melissa smiled. "Why yes agent um?"

"Traylor. Raelynn Traylor."

Melissa gave her a curt nod. "Agent Traylor we do have an

informant. That's why this meeting was called and your teams assembled. Surveillance, field work, wiretapping, and forensic accounting of Higgins's financials will all be centralized out of this branch office."

Raelynn glanced to the photos. What if Shane was the informant? Could he be working with them? Maybe?

"The ATF of course won't share who the informant is. Ian Higgins has evaded the law successfully for years. He's friends with the Mayor and vacations with your State Senator. I must stress the heightened level of discretion going forward," Melissa said, drawing Raelynn's attention back from her muddled thoughts. "Boys and girls this is why we will be putting each of you on several task forces. Agent Traylor since you seem very astute, I want you to work with Kevin Reyes. He's familiar with the gun trafficking that's tied to Ian Higgins's family in Ireland."

So that's the reason the ATF is here? Shane Lafferty has graduated from a bank robber to gun smuggler? I really know how to pick them.

Melissa walked back toward the front of the room, with her hands clasped behind her back. "Listen up. Our informant says that Ian Higgins has plans for the money he's stolen. The transport of weapons to Ireland will go down next week. So we have to work fast people. These men frequent a boxing gym named Gladiators. Ian Higgins is promoting the big fight next week. In forty-eight hours I want a complete update on your strategic plans for engagement. I want to know everything about this crew. Where they piss, shit, sleep, all of it. We require fieldwork. These guys are Irish Americans and very selective of the company they keep. Henry, Lily, Fredrick, you three will be canvassing the popular spots. The informant will get you the access to this inner circle as needed. Lily will continue to bartend at a bar called Foley's.

Raelynn's head shot up. She felt her chest tighten at the mention of Foley's. Lily didn't look familiar, but she was drinking that night. She slipped Lily a questioning look. The woman remained attentive and focused. Raelynn shifted in her chair uncomfortably. Maybe now was the time to make them aware of her run-in with Shane? *Maybe not.* Dammit what was she to do?

Raelynn stopped listening. She digested and silently fumed over the truth that was dropped in her lap. Shane Lafferty was a waste of a man who had turned to thievery, like the scumbag who shot her police officer father and condemned him to a life in a wheelchair. She loathed those that lived on the edge of society. *Then why did you pick him? You chose him Raelynn, and you knew what he was and wasn't the moment he walked into Foley's bar.* Why indeed. She had no clue what got into her last night, but she planned to correct that mistake and bring him to his knees if she had to.

"So looks like I'm your new shadow. Name is Kevin. My friends call me Ike."

A caramel hand extended from the sleeve of a very handsome black man standing over her. Raelynn removed the cap end of the pen she chewed on from her mouth. She glanced at the hand then up at the agent with a forced smile.

He wasn't bad on the eyes. A thin mustache goatee framed kissable lips. His skin was a smooth medium shade of brown. He had thick, dark, silky brows over chocolate drop eyes, the kind that a girl could get lost in. And his shoulders were broad and firm. Though he wore a standard suit and tie, she imagined him to be a runner. That's what came to mind. Him in sweats and a t-shirt, running long distances with granite tight abs, biceps, and marble hard thighs.

But sizing up his sex appeal in the first minute of a greeting was a bad idea, and she needed to make sure he didn't do the same with her. She wasn't conceited, and in fact she rarely noticed her own beauty. But dammit, every partner black, white or whatever would always make it a point to let his gaze linger on her curvy shape. Her breasts and her ass, no matter how she tried to cover them, constantly drew unwanted attention.

Her ex-boyfriend once told her that she had a coke-bottle figure fit for a life as a stripper not a Federal Agent. It pissed her off. She was more tomboy than girlie. Sex appeal, at least her own, meant nothing to her. Still the assessments of her physical attributes rang true, and were further confirmed by the lingering glances of every male partner she was put with.

Even her Section Chief had taken notice, and once assigned her to fieldwork where she had to dress like a call-girl to infiltrate a human sex trafficking ring. It was a good assignment but the gear she wore, and the way they paraded her in front of those scumbags to get them to catch the bait, never left the back of her mind. That's why she preferred Homeland Defense and true investigative assignments. Basically, these men did to her, what she had just done to Kevin Reyes in their first five seconds of meeting.

"Nice to meet you Kevin," she said in a very direct manner, refusing the offer to call him by the strange nickname, Ike. Shaking his hand she rose with the aid of his firm grip. "I think we should use today to read up on, um the case. How about an early start tomorrow?"

"Well… I was thinking we could start working with the team. Get to know our individual strengths, delegate and strategize."

"Great. See you tomorrow," she cut him off and ignored his request. She could feel his eyes on her during her hurried exit. Right now she needed to do some damage control. She'd be damned if all her hard work to survive Quantico, and land a branch office that wasn't in the cornfields of Iowa would blow up over this. If Shane was picked up and tried to bargain with the fact that he slept with her, she was toast. "Hey! Wait up!" Andy, her now former partner yelled after her. He walked fast behind her. She sighed, tossing the folders from the 'closed door debriefing' on her desk. Instead of acknowledging him she retrieved her laptop bag and started to shove the work inside.

"Did I hear right? Are you off the Muhammad case and working with the ATF?"

"News travels fast."

"Dammit Raelynn, we work together. Did you tell Greaves or Garrett that we're a good team? About what we've been doing?"

"Slow down," she said putting her purse on her shoulder. "They know, everyone knows about the case and what you've done."

"I can't sit behind this desk forever. I thought we were a team!" he said in a loud whisper, crowding her space in the cube. A hint of desperation sharpened his tone making it sound more like a whine.

Raelynn nodded in agreement. After all, she'd feel the same way if the roles were reversed. Andy O'Brian had been a strong partner. He worked equally as hard as she did. "I'll talk to Greaves." She glanced up to see Kevin in the hall talking to several others. His dark penetrating gaze lifted from the face of the chattering woman before him and locked with hers. He smirked. "Shit, I got to go."

"Go? Where?"

"Something came up. Um, cover for me. Okay?"

"No, stop… I want you to talk to Greaves!"

"Cover for me. I'll call you tonight and explain."

Quickly she grabbed her laptop and purse then fast walked to the elevator. It wasn't until the doors closed that she allowed herself to breathe. Dropping back against the wall she closed her eyes and focused.

She could turn this around. Bring the whole case to a close. The informant couldn't be as close to the truth as she could get with the help of Shane Lafferty.

A smile spread across her lips and an idea formed. A risky idea that would mean gambling her career, but if she could bring Shane Lafferty in, the score would propel her all the way to a Director's chair. She was sure of it. The doors opened and she rushed out. She knew exactly what she needed to do.

CHAPTER FOUR

Raelynn had circled the block twice. She only parked when she caught a familiar gleam from a side window of a passenger van positioned at the corner. It was a marked van. The standard Alice's Bakery insignia was scribbled along the side in mauve pink writing with rose cake decorations. She'd seen it on surveillance vans from her branch office before.

"Hmm, that was quick. I should have known." Raelynn reached in her glove compartment and pulled out mini binoculars. The front window of the van wasn't as heavily tinted. However, it showed no one inside the driver or passenger seat. This didn't mean it was the only surveillance team on the block.

Letting her engine idle she leaned forward and used the binoculars to scan the second level of the warehouse building it was parked in front of. She caught movement behind a foggy window, but nothing else. The front of the gym was definitely under surveillance.

Raelynn remembered a side entrance when she circled the block earlier. She tossed the binoculars to the passenger seat and shifted her rental into drive. Smoothly easing out onto the avenue she made another sweep, but parked a block further back along the alley.

Between a Subaru truck and a Corolla, her newly issued Ford Taurus fit snugly. The car was a loaner. Hers remained in the alley next to Foley's Bar. With all the drama, she'd gotten the rental that morning after having Andrea come pick her up. She needed to call her mechanic to make sure he picked up her ride.

Dismissing all doubts she focused on her goal. Time was short and she was taking a huge risk. Raelynn planned to approach Shane and feel him out. If he remained spooked because of her being a Federal agent then she'd give him some options. Of course she wasn't in a position to bargain for the agency, but she could sway a deal if Shane could deliver. The problem would be convincing Shane Lafferty to turn against his life of crime for her. A woman he had only had a one-night stand with.

Good luck with that Raelynn.

Checking her makeup in the mirror she took her time and steadied the hand that rubbed the rose-colored gloss brush over her bottom lip. She'd changed into a turtleneck and leather waist jacket with jeans. Throwing open the door she bristled and almost drew back to the warmth of her car against the unwelcoming chill.

How did a girl born and raised in sunny Pensacola, Florida end up in one of the coldest cities on the East Coast? She had wished for an assignment that would keep her close to her mother and her paraplegic dad. She missed them something awful, and regretted that her dreams to make her father proud had carried her further from home.

Raelynn was careful how she stepped along the icy sidewalk keeping her head low. Her choice in stiletto riding boots proved to be a foolish one, but she needed to look casual, blend in.

When she dashed into the Mediterranean restaurant called Shavo's, she could feel the soles of her feet slide on the polished floors. She begged forgiveness of the diners who looked up curiously and walked straight through the rows of tables to the back. Flashing her badge from her back pocket she slipped out of the back door. Gladiators did have a side entrance.

Raelynn stepped carefully toward it, her head turned upward so she could look for any sign of surveillance cameras. The ones from the street lamps out front were pointed to the front of the building, so this side entrance was in a blind spot to any of the surveillance teams or cameras positioned to the front of Gladiators.

You hope Raelynn, you know better than anyone that the Bureau is excellent at seeing while remaining unseen. What did Lily, the bartender at Foley's see? You, dancing the night away with the bank robber she was tailing?

The first problem presented itself quickly. The door she needed to enter the gym only opened from the inside. This meant she would have to wait until someone left, which could take a while, and time already wasn't on her side.

The second problem was going to be far more complicated. After she entered, she would need to get to Shane and talk to him without drawing anyone's suspicion. If an agent was inside they might recognize her. Again, the risks did little to douse her ambition or arrogance. She removed her phone and dialed the agency.

Quickly, she left a message for her Section Chief advising him that she thought she'd follow up on a possible lead. She would blame her rushed behavior on wanting to get a jump on the case. However, she would be careful of being seen. Shane needed to be able to trust her, that in itself would be a hard sale if he was guilty of what she believed he was.

The door opened. An athletic man in jeans, wearing a hoodie and carrying a gym bag emerged. She sashayed toward him and he paused.

"Thanks," she winked, putting more of a sway into her hips when she passed him. Either he was too stunned or too cold to follow up on her unexplained side door entrance. Once inside Gladiators her confidence rose with the temperature. Several heads of muscled men in sweaty sleeveless t-shirts and long shorts turned her way. None seemed friendly, but a woman in their midst had them all watching her curiously. The gym was like any other. Along the walls were hanging punching bags. Several workout benches were occupied. A few men were paired off, while others jumped rope or shadowboxed.

In the center was a boxing ring. Most were drawn from their own workouts, to the four corners of the ring, to observe in silence as two men sparred, donning headgear and gloves. Raelynn focused on the taller one of the two. When he threw the next punch she saw the shamrock tattoo on his thick neck and knew him immediately. It was Shane.

Raelynn crossed her arms and admired his technique. He was light on his feet, jabbing and ducking punches then slamming his opponent in the face with counter swings. All of it left her heart racing. She loved his moves, the way his sweat glistened over taut muscles, all of it. He and the other man circled each other in the ring, careful to only deliver critical blows. Shane was definitely the better of the two.

Shane threw another commanding punch and the sparring partner was knocked on his back—flat. A short stocky man with a cap pulled down low on a shaggy head, parted the ropes and climbed in the ring. He started yelling at Shane, shoving him back. Apparently the blow was too decisive. Shane spit out his mouth guard and stormed out of the ring with a few expletives of his own.

"Okay girl, showtime," Raelynn mumbled under her breath.

She strutted across the gym and headed straight for him. At first he didn't notice, but others did. A few spoke their displeasure at her sudden appearance in a guy's arena when she passed. That's when he looked up. He froze, watching her approach. A shadow of a frown darkened his face and her heart sank. He didn't look happy at all to see her.

What did she expect? The man ran from her. Clearly a federal agent showing up unannounced to his playground wasn't his idea of a pleasant thing.

"Shane Lafferty," she said smiling.

Shane narrowed his gaze on her. "What you doing here?"

"Came to see you," she said.

"Look, I'm busy, I don't have time for this."

"I suggest you make time for me Shane."

He turned and looked at her. A muscle in his jaw flicked angrily. She didn't like that look. Was he seriously trying to blow her off? No way in hell. "Like I said, not a good time sweetheart. Leave a number with Rich over there and I'll call you later."

Raelynn's head turned in the direction of his nod. She saw a scrawny kid with ear buds in his ears, flipping through a magazine while sitting on a barstool near the front doors. When she turned back to Shane he was gone.

Raelynn fumed, watching as he walked out of the gym through double doors. The guy slamming his fists into the red and white weight bag next to her looked over and chuckled. She shot him a steely look and he threw his hands up in mock surrender. "Nothing personal beautiful, but Shane's in one of his moods. Not likely to change over a sweet piece of ass."

"Well I'm more than a sweet piece of ass, and I don't take well to being dismissed." She turned and marched straight through the doors Shane disappeared through. Her impulsive pursuit delivered her into a locker room. The steam from the showers, and musk from those shedding their sweats and shirts, hit her hard. Her steps slowed. She pressed her lips together in a thin determined line.

What the hell am I doing? Raelynn couldn't help but notice the buff naked men with towels over their necks heading in and out of the showers. Two of them gave her challenging looks, cocks hanging. None of them approached. Most didn't seem fazed or shocked by her presence. She sucked down a breath of confidence and strolled through the large locker room, nodding at a few men as she passed by. He couldn't have undressed that quickly. She was right. He was standing in the third row of lockers, sans shirt, with a towel tied around his waist, unraveling the tape around his knuckles.

"You and I need to talk."

"About?" Shane asked. Turning to his locker he removed a

large black duffle bag.

"You know damn well what about. Now do you want to have that conversation here?"

"Do you?" he cast his gaze back over his shoulder. There was a look of smugness on his face she wanted to demolish. Raelynn evened her tune. "Last night was a mistake."

"Tell me about it." He mumbled, and then dropped his towel. His eyes clung to hers, analyzing her reaction. Raelynn summoned control over the urge to lower her gaze and acknowledge his hanging cock. She blinked feeling a little lightheaded at being held under his stare this way.

"I know who you are Shane." Raelynn cleared her throat. "When you ran out last night, I um, made a point to look you up. You're a career criminal. Got it from your father. Right?"

"I don't need a 'this is your life' lesson from you Raelynn."

"I know what you need."

"Really?" A sudden icy contempt flashed in his eyes.

Raelynn chose to ignore it. For now. She blinked then refocused her gaze. "What you need is an opportunity. Am I right? A chance to turn your life around? Hell maybe you don't. Either way we need to talk about what happened last night." Raelynn stepped closer. A guy behind her grumbled something about women in the showers. "You talk to me or I'll tell these men in here who I am, and how close you are to the Feds."

"Really? You want to go there?" he challenged.

She wavered because she didn't.

"You get one chance at this Shane. One. Then I'm done." She

managed to reply through stiff lips.

"Have dinner with me."

"What?" Raelynn's brows drew downward in a frown.

"Dinner. You do eat?"

"No."

"Then bye." He grabbed his towel and headed past the bench.

"Wait!"

Shane waited. His mouth twisted with impatience when she didn't say anything. He spoke in a low almost pleading voice. "Get out of here and don't come back. I know what this is about. I'm your little secret. You don't want your reputation tarnished with the likes of me right? You want to give me some line of bullshit about how you can help me go straight. Well you got me wrong darling. Nothing crooked about me Rae."

"My name is Raelynn." She grunted.

He gave her a sardonic smile that sent her pulse racing. "Why are you here?"

"I need you to trust me. I can help you."

"You want my trust then you need to earn it."

"Are you insane?" Nervously she moistened her dry lips.

"Maybe I am, have dinner with me and we'll discuss it."

"I will not. This isn't about some hook-up. It's about more than that and you know it."

"Then it's on you babe. Dinner. Meet me at Clery's on Dartmouth Street. Around eight and I'll hear you out." The smile in his eyes contained a sensuous flame. He stepped closer. But she stepped back frowning. He stiffened under the pending rejection, she could sense everything about him tighten with tension. A wry but indulgent glint appeared in his eyes as he waited for her answer.

"I can't have dinner with you dammit. And you know why!" She had to step further back from his bare, hard chest now eye level with her face.

"Then to hell with your offer. See you when I see you."

"Shane!" she shouted in a loud whisper.

He headed away.

"Dammit!" she huffed. She tried to follow but stopped.

Again it registered exactly where she was. Her gaze swept the other men, a few met her stare. Shane tossed his towel over a ceramic grey, tiled, four-foot wall.

He walked barefoot between men showering on either side of the open stall. His backside was almost as glorious as his front. A firm ass, muscled thighs, and calves with a hint of hair that lay wavy to the back of his legs. Raelynn swallowed down the excitement blooming in her chest. This attraction between them would be perilous if she wasn't careful. She watched with a stilted breath, while he turned a large silver dial and brought down a pour from the showerhead. He tilted his head back, sending rivulets of water over his hard pecks and the rigid angles of his torso. The stream rinsed through his thick dark pubic hair and drained off his languid cockhead.

Raelynn licked her lips remembering how nice his cock was in her mouth, and on her tongue. She could barely swallow him, but she gave it her best shot last night.

Her gaze slowly climbed up his athletic form. He rolled his neck then opened his eyes and fastened the sexiest stare on her body, while he lathered his cock with long strokes. A challenge it's both raw and full of wicked promise.

Raelynn felt heat flood her cheeks, warming her neck and chest with embarrassment. Her body ached for his touch. The smoldering flame she saw burning in his irises as he lathered his chest made her crave the impossible. Dinner? Hell, a girl did have to eat.

Shane smirked at her weakness. Was she that damn pathetic?

"Look lady I don't know how you got back here but you have to go. Now!" the short trainer barked at her, his arms flapped excitedly. Raelynn agreed with the man. She needed air. She couldn't breathe.

When she glanced back at Shane she discovered he had dismissed her, continuing to shower, now with his back turned. She gave up. Raelynn left the way she came.

How the hell was she supposed to pull off dinner? The fresh air cleared her head. He's an arrogant bastard, a criminal, not worth the energy or risk. What if someone in the gym was undercover and saw her follow him into the showers?

She was losing control. It was time to end this cat and mouse game between them. After all, she didn't know who he was when they slept together, her Deputy Director would understand. Maybe she should just confess. Confess to what, having a life? Dumb. Dumb. Dumb.

Or she could turn this around. All the way around. Pull him in, gain true insight into Higgins's organization. *Yeah, yeah, you keep saying that but the odds are he'd be the one turning you around, bending you over and slamming all seven inches from last night into you until you broke. Walk away Rae, no better yet run…*

Raelynn closed her eyes trying to convince herself to listen to her inner voice and not make the most reckless move of her career. She saw his smirk, his piercing blue eyes. She shivered in remembrance of the timbre of his voice when he disobeyed her. She couldn't deny part of her, a very small part, wanted to protect him. Which only infuriated her more. Feeling her phone buzz she snatched it off her hip.

"Agent Traylor."

"Glad you answered."

"Who is this?" Raelynn squinted.

"Kevin Reyes. Your new partner, remember?"

Raelynn headed back through the restaurant to her car.

"What is it? What do you want?"

"Huh? Maybe we got off on the wrong foot."

Raelynn eased into the driver's seat of her car. She slammed the car door then counted down her frustration before softening her tone. "Of course not, forgive me. I apologize, it's just been a day."

"I totally understand. I'm the new guy; you have a partner already so the transition is weird. I get it."

"Yeah, um, whatever. Something up?" she asked starting the car.

"I spoke to the Director and learned a few things. I think there are two men we should focus on. Names given to us by the informant."

Her stomach dropped. She closed her eyes. "The names?"

"Shane and Scott Lafferty. Cousins. Our source says they were likely the perps to hit the bank. More interesting is this Shane Lafferty, he was once a contender for a heavyweight championship. Kid had a short run, but I remember him."

"Really?" she said dryly.

He kept going. "I got a lead that his rematch to claim the title is the big fight Ian Higgins is backing."

"So why would he rob banks?" Raelynn asked, taking her hand off the gearshift.

"Who knows? He's been in a few scrapes in his early twenties but cleaned up his act about five years ago. He lost a title, a belt, then withdrew. His comeback is all over Sports Center. Maybe it's money issues. Either way, we need to make a trip."

"Where?"

"Georgia, his father is a lifer on a double murder rap in the Penitentiary. I think we can get something useful from him."

Raelynn sat there with the car idling. She gripped the steering wheel.

"You there agent Traylor?"

"Yes, what time do you want to leave?"

"Seven in the morning. Got a jet for our disposal. I've already arranged the meeting with the warden. They'll bring him in when we arrive."

"I'll see you at seven." Raelynn hung up. She sat there another second watching the faces leaving and arriving at Gladiators. There was nothing to do but handle it, get into the case and bust Ian Higgins.

CHAPTER FIVE

Shane rolled his shoulders. He cracked his knuckles once more, and then began to pace again. Cass forced him to wait it out. Well he didn't have time for a lecture. The stakes were high now.

Raelynn not only came here, but he was pretty sure she knew all about being his alibi for the robbery. He was too hard on her. He should have heard her out. Maybe, just maybe she could get him out of the deep well of shit he drowned in.

Higgins wanted him to throw the fight as his final repayment. Afterwards he'd let Scotty go, leave Margene alone and finally allow Shane to live out the rest of his miserable existence in peace. However, it also meant his career as a boxer would be over.

It took a lot of work and fenagalin to get him in the ring with the Champ. He took a dive and he'd be a laughing stock all over again. If he were to believe Higgins's threat, he and Scotty would get tagged for the bank job and off to prison they'd go if he didn't throw the fight.

Shane did believe him though. The man vacationed with Senators. Shane was just some washed up boxer with a theft record as long as the lies he'd told throughout his life. Who would the Feds believe?

"Damn it!" he swung a punch at nothing.

A raw and primitive rage gripped him. He grunted deep in his chest. Why was he so fucking stupid? Now he was caught with nowhere to turn. The door opened. Cass walked in ignoring him. The sixty-year-old boxing trainer, and mentor to the lost, looked tired. Extremely tired.

"About what happened in the ring with Danny."

"You smoking again?" Cass barked.

"A little, not much."

"The cigarettes have to go. You're in training. Or have you forgotten?" Cass waved off his excuse. "Sit Shane."

"I really can't stay back. I have to…"

"Got work to do for Ian Higgins?" Cass asked, his gaze lifting to meet Shane's. A shock of defeat rendered Shane mute. The judgment in Cass's eyes assailed him with a terrible sense of bitterness over being born a Lafferty. Cass shook his head accepting Shane's silence as an admission of guilt. "Word has it you're back on his payroll. That you might have had something to do with that robbery the other day."

"Not true."

"If I heard about it Shane, how long before the cops do too? Dammit you said you'd stay clean. I believed you when you told me that you came back for the title, and this time you'd see it through. This makes no sense!"

"It's not true. Whatever you heard is not true."

"Don't lie to me boy! You're in trouble!" Cass slammed his fist on the top of the desk. He glared at Shane, incensed.

"You left and I understood," Cass began, "When you showed up here three months ago saying you wanted to get your life back I agreed. Even though I knew it would take at least a year to return you to the ring in the condition you once were, I agreed. Now I believe in you again, and look at what you've done!"

"It's complicated Cass."

"If Higgins has his claws in you then forget the re-match. Walk away. Now. Forget Margene, forget Scott and the shit he's always mixed up in. Just leave Shane before it's too late."

"You know I can't do that," he picked up his duffle. "Some things are beyond your control, and now mine as well."

"What does that mean?"

"The fight goes down, as Higgins wants. You know what that means, don't pretend you haven't done this with fighters before," he mumbled. Leaving Cass's office he felt tired. The choices he's made, good or bad, he always had a reason for making them. Now he felt nothing, he had no reasons.

If he had been more focused on his surroundings he would have noticed the shadows behind him once he exited the side entrance to head for his motorcycle. Instead his mind flashed back to Raelynn. Seeing her again had really thrown him. He envisioned their next encounter to be with her behind her badge, and him in handcuffs. She however, was as bold today as she was last night when she gave herself to him.

It took balls to walk into the showers the way she did. Shane smirked to himself. He remembered the defiance in her cute face, the way she stood up to him. He found himself smiling, but only briefly. The sharp sting of her words echoed in his conscious mind. She said she knew who he was. That meant Higgins wasn't paranoid. The Feds were sniffing around. Dammit.

"Shane. I owe you something."

Shane turned directly into a fist. The blow hit him dead center in the face so ferociously he feared it would split his skull. Before he could recover another person grabbed his arms and pinned them behind his back. His assailant swung again, delivering double punches to the gut. Shane felt bile rise to his throat as his insides crushed inward. He struggled to maintain consciousness but the beating continued, more direct hits to the face and head as the person wailed on him with what felt like a sledgehammer.

"Let him go! Now!"

Shane dropped to his knees. He spit blood, gasping, gagging.

"Who the fuck are you lady?" he heard a man say. The voice sounded familiar. He lifted his head. Blood in one eye clouded his vision, but he saw Mickey standing next to Danny, his sparring partner from the match earlier. Raelynn stepped between the men with a gun.

"You stay a minute longer and you'll find out who the fuck I am."

"Hey? She was in the gym earlier Mick. I think she's with Shane."

"You protecting this piece of shit?" Mickey coughed up a wad of phlegm and spat on Shane.

Shane shook off his delirium. He tried to rise but staggered. He needed to rise. He'd murder Mickey with his own two hands.

He heard the release click on a gun, when he dropped to his side he saw the weapon. Raelynn held it directly dead center to Mickey's forehead. Her voice was controlled with deadly calm, but no one doubted the words she spoke. "You got three minutes to disappear, or I'll pull this trigger and make it permanent."

Mickey was a punk. There was no way in hell he attacked him with his fists. Shane searched for the source and spotted it not far from where he lay. A pipe, covered with his blood, lay a few feet before him. The cowardly bastard was trying to kill him. "I'll kill you!" Shane growled.

He heard a litany of curses, then hard footfalls of running. He lifted his head once more and saw no one but her. Raelynn stooped. With the face of an angel she stared down at him. "You're hurt Shane. I need to get you to a hospital."

"No. I'm fine. Leave."

"I won't leave you here." She reached for him.

"Go. Now. Just leave me."

"No. C'mon, you're coming with me."

"Wait, Rae, I can't go to a hospital." He said struggling to remain conscious. "You want to help me then prove it. Don't take me to a hospital. Just get me the hell out of here."

She was strong despite her petite, curvaceous frame. He felt her lifting him and found the strength to stand. She grabbed his bag, and he dropped his arm around her to keep from slipping back to the ground. When her arm eased around his waist it felt right. She felt right. "I do want to help you. Trust me. My car is down the street. We need to go through this restaurant out to the other side."

"What—no, just get me to my bike, I can manage…"

"Shane, listen to me. They have the gym under surveillance. I can't be seen with you. Your bike is parked to the front of the alley. Now let's go this way," she said more firmly.

Shocked, that she'd even bother after how he treated her, he simply nodded. Was she really helping him? No fucking way was she helping him. He half expected to see a SWAT team waiting for him.

Together they took the side door into the eatery and surprised several of the people working in the kitchen. Raelynn guided him out and then through the door. Her car, a different car, was parked in a lot down the street.

Walking, or better yet staggering, was hard. Shane felt as if his head was split open. The wound to the left side of his face streamed blood down his temple and jaw. Ruby droplets dripped on his shirt. That's why the people were staring.

Raelynn forced him to walk, and walk fast. The cold wind slamming against them was the only thing that kept him from giving into the need to slip under. And when she deposited him in the back seat of her car his conscious mind shorted. "Thanks babe," Was the last thing he heard himself say, before darkness slipped in.

***

'Jesus! Jesus! Jesus H. Christ!' Raelynn hit the steering wheel. She glanced in the rearview mirror and saw Shane bleeding and unconscious in the back seat. It all happened so fast. She decided to wait him out. Explain to him the benefit in turning himself in. The problem was her parking spot gave her little or no advantage to seeing him when he left.

It was fate that timed her arrival, just as he was being beaten to death. All she had planned to do was to take him into the bureau herself and make sure he got a fair deal. To her horror they were trying to kill him. One guy hit him so hard in the head with a pipe he should be dead.

She glanced up in the mirror. *Was he dead?*

"What should I do? What should I do?"

You know what to do Raelynn. Take him to the hospital and leave him there. Get out of this mess now, while you still have an option.

Shane begged her not to take him to the hospital. He was a tough guy, and he didn't look easily spooked. If he feared the hospital there was good reason. Higgins could easily get to him while she struggled to explain to her superiors why she found him and knew him. What choice did she really have? What if the men that were beating him alerted Higgins and he discovered who she was. It would be the end of Shane and blow the entire investigation out of the water.

So where will you take him Raelynn? The man is bleeding all over your back seat.

She couldn't take him home, though she had his address from her intel. Her place? No, no, she couldn't use her place. Someone would see. Her nosey neighbor Adalene was always perched in her window like a cat.

"Shit!" she reached for her cell phone and dialed Andrea.

"Wsup chic!" Andrea said, her voice cheery as ever.

"I need a favor."

"Okay, name it. Oh wait. Girl I forgot to tell you when I

picked you up this morning. Something went down with the guy at the bar. The cute guy, his name was George. Anyways wanted to hook up, after we made out in my car. I didn't want you saying I was reckless and all. We going too…"

"Andrea focus! Listen to me. Your rental home over in Cambridge, it's empty right?"

"Yep."

"I need to um, crash there tonight."

"What? Why?"

"No questions, okay? Can I use it?"

"Sure. I have the key in the usual spot. You know where it is. Rae, are you okay?"

"Fine. I'm fine. I just need to cool off. I want to be alone. You know?"

"Then why not go home? Is it Eddie? Is he trying to get back with you?"

"Yeah, um, yes. That's what it is. Eddie, you know he won't stop. So I'm going to use your place to relax."

"Okay, let's make it a girl's night I can bring over some music and wine."

"No! Just want to be alone. You understand?"

"Sure, I guess. Well call if you need anything."

"Bye, love you." Raelynn hung up. If Shane died on her she was dead meat. *You should take him to the hospital.* Raelynn pounded her hand on the steering wheel. The men in the alley saw her face. How long before Ian Higgins placed her and the entire investigation blew up? "Dammit!"

She drove up the interstate and accelerated.

***

"Wake up!"

Shane felt a hard shake. He opened his eyes to an unforgiving headache. It was as if someone had poured lava into his skull and set his brain no fire. Raelynn tugged on him. She tried to make him rise. He had slumped over in the back seat. Using his right hand he pushed himself and sat upright. She wasn't letting go though. She pulled on his sleeve. "We have to get inside. Now."

"Inside where?" he groaned.

"Never mind it. Come on. Now."

Sadly he had no choice. He couldn't get his bearings. With her help he eased out of the backseat and stood on shaky legs. The joints in his knees went to jelly and he slumped back against the open car door. His head hurt so bad he didn't even realize there were shocking jolts of painful cramping in his gut and under his ribs. "What happened?" he asked confused.

"Shane c'mon." Raelynn grunted pulling him up and easing her arm around his waist. Together they staggered to the front door of a house he didn't know. Shane managed to turn his head. There were many houses, manicured lawns, a dog in a neighbor's yard barking. He was somewhere else? Why?

"Where are we?"

"Some place we can fix you up. Talk."

This babe didn't listen well. He had no intention of talking to a Fed. But he held on to her. He liked the feel of her body against him. She soothed him. They went inside. It was a cottage style home where the living room and kitchen were to the front, and a dining room and bonus room was to the back. He saw a purple velvet chair and dropped in it. Raelynn closed and locked the door. She shed her leather waist jacket. In doing so he noticed the blood on the front of her shirt. *How bad am I hurt?*

"Shane. Look at me." she said gingerly holding his face. "Stay with me okay? I'm going to get you something for your head."

He grabbed her wrist when she drew away. Raelynn paused, she waited, expectantly patient. He wanted to ask her so many things. Why was she doing this? What was her angle? Did she really want to help him? None of that came out. Instead he grunted: "Thanks."

She nodded and drew away. He leaned forward. It felt as if the heaviness in his skull would make his head roll off his shoulders. To his relief his head remained attached, but the pain split him in two. Shane, the man who can handle it, and Shane, the boy that wanted to cry out in agony. He doubted his injuries were serious.

As a boxer he was used to taking a beating around his head. Growing up as the only child of Margene and Calvin Lafferty he'd built up a tolerance to physical pain. He groaned, and the man in him won out. Shane managed to shed his leather jacket. Next he reached to the back of his neck, grabbed the collar of his sweatshirt and gently pulled it over his head and off. It smelled of the rank alley he collapsed in. All energy spent, Shane closed his eyes and lowered back into the comfy chair. He soon felt a cool compress to his forehead. It was like she opened his skull and poured ice cubes into it. "Owe," he groaned.

"Hold still."

Raelynn wiped the blood from his forehead and the side of his face. "It's pretty bad, the swelling is, but the cut isn't deep. Maybe you should go to the hospital. If you lose consciousness again, I'm taking you."

"I can handle it. I've been hit harder."

"Boxing?" she asked.

His gaze lifted and his eyes locked with hers. Should he tell her that his father had once used his face as a punching bag when he was a kid? Should he tell her of the many street fights he had as a kid that made him crave the violence of a boxing ring? "Yeah, boxing," he lied.

"I'll stitch it for you," She sat on the coffee table and placed a white and red first aid box in her lap. She opened the lid and removed some medical gauze, tape, and a surgical needle.

"What? You a doctor now?" Shane chuckled.

Raelynn didn't smile. In fact she looked pissed. Shane had definitely blown it with this one. Still he couldn't deny that part of him felt at ease with her near. She had that effect on him. His life was shit, but he could forget that for a moment now. "I'm fine. I needed a minute to get my bearings. I'll go. Just tell me where we are," he said and tried to lift. A bout of dizziness gripped him and forced him back down.

"You aren't going anywhere." She fixed him with a hard glare.

Shane chuckled. "You holding me hostage?"

Raelynn slammed the lid down on the safety kit. She stood and put her hands to her curvy hips. Not many women can wear jeans the way this one could. She had nice hips and a round ass, thick and bubbly. Her slim, trim waistline, and ample bosom that hovered above him spoke of femininity and softness. It was dark the night he touched those curves. He saw her body, but not the way he had wanted to. If he ever got another shot at her, he'd fuck with the lights on.

"Shane."

Her voice forced his gaze to lift from her crotch and lock with hers.

"I want answers. Did you know who I was when you came into Foley's?"

"I thought you were going to stitch me up? Going to hold back medical attention while you interrogate me?"

She looked down to her hands and realized she held the needle and thread. Sighing she came forward, bringing her fresh powdery scent with her. Shane inhaled her and leaned into the back cushion.

"Hold still." She dabbed at the weeping wound on his face. He winced but managed.

"Did you know who I was at Foley's?" she asked in a calmer tone.

"Huh?"

"When you approached me on the dance floor. Did you know who I was? Was this Higgins's plan? Get an agent in the bed then try to flip her or something?"

Shane chuckled. "Owe!"

"Don't laugh at me." She warned. He realized the pain was inflicted on purpose. He held still and relaxed as the needle and thread went through his skin stitch by stitch.

"So I planned your flat tire? You offering to take me home for the night was all on me?"

Shane's gaze lifted. Raelynn looked down at him. "Don't

wrinkle your brow, I can't finish."

He lowered his gaze. She finished after a few stitches then leaned over to get a pair of scissors on the coffee table, and snipped the string. "Here's the thing Shane Lafferty. I can believe last night was random. Stuff happens. We happened. I'll be damned if something this random turns my career."

"You haven't broken any laws. Fucking a criminal is perfectly legal."

"But you have!" she stepped back. Her beautiful covered breasts rose and fell with the deep angry breaths she released. "How long do you think you can go on with this life of crime and not have it catch up to you? Those men that attacked you were trying to kill you. Don't you want out of this? I read that you were once a good boxer. You're trying to be a good one again, but you can't if you don't do something drastic to get out of this mess. Every good deed deserves a reward, do one and I'll do one for you. Unburden yourself Shane."

"What are you the morality police?" he half chuckled. "Who says I committed a crime? So what I have a record, most men I know do. I'm a boxer, and that fight was just some argument in the gym that spilled out into the streets. You saw me yesterday. I was coming back from an interview. Trying to get a job. Failed at it. Then I got to dance with you, hold you, the only crime I committed was leaving your bed when you asked me not to."

He needed to throw her off of his scent. Not to save his own ass, but hers. Not even her badge could protect her from Ian Higgins. The man had people on his payroll everywhere. What was she some rookie agent? Had to be, to take the risks of trying to flip him on her own. It was time to send this beauty back to the life she belonged to and far away from his shit. This story won't end well for either of them if he doesn't.

"You're lying," she said with distaste.

"Prove it."

He held her angry stare. He wasn't going to win her over this way. Maybe he should try another approach. "The past is the past Raelynn."

"No it's not. I'm the Federal agent that will probably be putting handcuffs on you by the end of the week. Do you hear me? You're in trouble and it's in my best interest, and yours that we stop all the games and you allow me to help you."

"Help me? How?"

"We meet with my boss. You confess and tell him everything about Ian Higgins's operation, and the robbery of First National yesterday. Become a Federal witness and testify against him. If we get a conviction I guarantee the agency will give you a new start. A new identity."

"No."

"It's a good offer."

"Not one you can make. What are you? A desk agent? Trying to make it up the ranks? I'm not stupid sweetheart. You aren't working out a deal for me, you're trying to hustle me to get one for you."

"Me? That's ridiculous," she marched her sexy ass back to the kitchen to possibly wash her hands free of his blood.

He tried to push up but a wave of nausea knocked him back down. "Here's my promise to you Rae. Last night never happened. I don't know you and you don't know me. Let's leave it at that." He sighed, gripped the chair arms with both hands, and forced himself to lift from the cushion seat.

"Where do you think you're going?" she asked, returning with a glass of water and a pill bottle.

"Call me a cab. Never mind, where's my bag, my phone's in it. I'll call someone to pick me up. I know a place I can crash, keep a low profile until I feel better."

"I thought it was just a gym fight. Why the need to keep a low profile?"

"You know what I mean."

"Why not let me take you to the hospital so you can get checked out if you're such a law abiding citizen."

"Rae, babe, let it go. For your own good!" he shouted back at her.

"My name is Raelynn, and I'm not your babe!" she shouted back at him.

"You were last night."

"Asshole."

He smiled.

Raelynn set the glass on the coaster on the coffee table. She pressed a hand to his shoulder and forced him to sit back. Shane's gaze arched up to her kind face. For a minute she just stared into his eyes. When she blinked his heart actually fluttered. There was an invitation in the smoldering brown depths of her eyes. To trust her, believe her lame offer. But he knew Ian Higgins, he'd kill them both using the same hand of the law she claimed could protect them. And that was a problem. Mickey had seen her face. She drew a gun on him. That would get back. Now her life was in jeopardy. The instinct to protect her was so strong he felt his chest swell.

"I brought you some aspirin," she said softly, drawing her hand from his, turning to the coffee table, and picking up the glass and aspirin. "Here."

He accepted the glass and the three blue pills.

"Get comfortable Shane. We aren't leaving here until you start listening. I want to help you."

Before he could object she was gone. He didn't' have the strength to fight with her. Though secretly part of him enjoyed the attention.

Stitching his forehead wasn't hard to do. She'd learned that skill and a few other things in Quantico. Keeping her hands steady and her mind focused when touching him was something different. Raelynn was no fool. Any dalliance with Shane Lafferty would end in disaster. She still couldn't decide if she liked him. Sure she lusted for him, but he was a criminal. A fact she often forgot when he stared at her.

He had beautiful eyes. They gleamed with interest under his dreamy lids every time she spoke to him. They followed her every movement. One look into the sexy pair and she dreamed of being crushed beneath him. The attraction between them was disturbing to her in every way. Not because of any pre-conceived notions that it could be more than sex. But because she, Raelynn Carol Traylor, would risk all these years of hard work over sex.

Washing her hands she avoided her reflection in the mirror.

She kept telling herself that she could handle the stumbles she's made in the past 24 hours. But now she had her doubts.

"Rae?"

She turned from the sink to find Shane leaning against the doorframe; he had a pack of cigarettes in his hand. He pulled out a slender white cigarette and put it between pressed lips.

"I told you my name is Raelynn," she said snatching the pack of cigarettes and the one from his mouth away. He blinked at her, surprised. "No smoking in here. It's a filthy habit. I don't like it."

"To me you're Rae." He stated flatly. He watched amused as she flushed his cigarettes down the toilet. She tossed the empty pack into the trash and dusted her hands.

"Look I need my bag. I need to um, make some calls," he said.

"No."

"No?" his voice pitched high.

She crossed her arms. "You heard me. No calls, no nothing. Not until we figure out the next step. Besides those men aren't done with you, I'm sure."

"I can take care of myself."

"All the same, those are my rules."

Shane forced himself out of his lean. She could see how shaky he was on his feet and the urge to return to help him stand almost made her act. But he withdrew and staggered away.

Raelynn followed. To her surprise he had her keys and was headed to the door. "Hey! I told you no!"

"I'll be back."

Raelynn hurried after him. She watched him from the front

porch, flip open the trunk of her car. She waited while he made a phone call he didn't want her to hear. Apparently he was recovering quickly. He paced by the car, talking with his head low. He then slammed the trunk, slipped the phone in his pocket and started toward her.

She stepped back and let him inside. "Trouble?"

"Does it matter?"

Raelynn closed the door. "We started out wrong Shane. I approached this wrong. Let's start again. Really talk."

"We tried that. Clearly we see things differently."

"So you're a boxer?" she asked dropping on the sofa. He paused then sat next to her. There was a comfortable distance between them. Raelynn appreciated it. "I saw you in the ring. You're good. You almost won a belt too? Right?"

He smirked, staring at her.

"I could find almost everything on you from grade school up until then. What I can't figure out is what happened to you for two years? And why return to work for Ian Higgins?"

"So you always wanted to be the law?" he asked slumping down into the sofa cushion. Raelynn frowned. She sighed and relaxed. "Yes, my dad was a police officer."

"Was?" Shane asked.

"A thief... a man shot him. He's in a wheelchair. He interrupted a robbery."

"I'm sorry to hear that."

"Yeah, me too," she said but the bitterness in her tone could not be disguised.

"So that explains it."

"Explains what?"

"Why you look at me like that. You think I'm scum, like the man who shot your father?"

"I don't know you Shane. So I don't know what to think. You won't tell me anything."

"My father's a lifer. In the penitentiary for a double homicide. My mother's an alcoholic that thinks she's twenty-five instead of fifty-five. I've known Ian Higgins all my life and he…"

Raelynn waited. Shane didn't look at her when he spoke. He focused somewhere else. Sitting on the edge of her seat, she sat waiting, hoping for something revealing, something she could use. She held her breath. But he didn't speak. He just sat there. Any mention of Ian Higgins put Shane on automatic shutdown. Was the man that frightening?

"Who did your father kill?" She tried shifting the conversation to something he might discuss.

"What did it say in his file?"

"I didn't read about your father. I was more interested in you," she said softly.

To this Shane's head turned. He glanced at her. "What are we doing here Rae? You don't have to worry about me giving you up. I already told you that. But you can't crack me sweetheart. I have nothing to lose and nothing to gain by helping you go after Ian Higgins. I'm a lost cause."

"I don't think so." Surprised that what she said was true, she averted her gaze. Raelynn sensed it last night when he walked into

Foley's. Behind his hard exterior she believed there was a noble cause. Her father taught her to see with her heart as well as her mind when dealing people. That's what would separate her from the other agents who were strictly textbook. Her heart said that Shane didn't quite fit the mold. There was something more to him. It made her search for excuses to help. No, this wasn't just about self-preservation.

"I think you've had a bad deal from day one. Could it be that you are caught up in something bigger than you? I swear I never do what... um, we are different. Not color I mean. We're different because our opportunities were. Talk to me. Tell me something."

"I want you."

She frowned. "What?"

His gaze dropped from her face to her shoulders then to her breasts. "You want to know something, well there you have it. I want you. Again."

"Sex? Are you kidding me?"

"It's a good tension breaker. Conversation starter."

Raelynn laughed. "So I get it. You don't want to talk, you don't want my help, you just want sex. Shane, let's get one thing straight. Last night was a one-time event. I'd rather join you and rob a bank than sleep with you again." She rose from the sofa. She could feel his heated glare on her back. But she refused to take the accusation back. Time was up. She wasn't going to play around with this any longer. "I'll fix us something to eat. Looks like we'll be here for awhile. Why don't you take the time to consider my offer, again."

Raelynn headed to the kitchen.

CHAPTER SIX

The best she could pull together for dinner was a few cans of beef stew and some stale crackers. The place wasn't quite lived in and the cabinets were all but bare. She did however find a ten-year-old bottle of Chianti from Andrea's visit to Italy years ago.

She poured, they ate, and she put on the charm. Raelynn tried talking to him about sports, politics, the weather, anything to get him to open up to her. Mostly he stared at her or her breasts, and made a few passing remarks about corruption with the re-gentrification of South Boston. Once the bottle of wine was done, so was she.

Raelynn offered to take him home. To her surprise he declined. It seemed that Shane wasn't as hurried as before to escape their little setup. His reasoning was sound however, they both had too much to drink to get on the road. So they agreed to crash and she'd drive him back before dawn.

When Shane relaxed in the den in front of the TV, surfing for a channel he wanted to watch, Raelynn became a bit nervous. She spent a half hour cleaning to pass the time. It gave her a chance to process the meaning of the day, and her next move. When she was done she realized how exhausted she was.

The day had wiped her out. The wine made her lethargic, sleepy. That's why she decided on the warm bath. She felt sticky and bone weary under her clothes. A nice soak in the tub, then a few hours of sleep would work. Then she'd take Shane Lafferty back and shut down the part of her brain that thought this whole thing was a good idea. After all she wasn't his guardian angel. Hell they weren't even friends. Why should she bother with a man who couldn't be bothered to save himself?

Raelynn slipped deep into the warm bath and closed her eyes. The steam off the water opened her pours, and single trickles of sweat coursed down her temples and the bridge of her nose. It was divine.

The door to the bathroom creaked as it opened with a dry squeak that woke her from her comfortable haze. Her fatigue heavy lids parted a fraction to see Shane stick his head inside. Their eyes met for a brief moment. The bath water was absent of suds to cover her nudity. Her body was partially in view in the murky water, her dark nipples bobbed above the surface. He noticed. Raelynn said nothing. When caught in his heated gaze she lost all sense of modesty.

"I want to talk." He came inside.

"Now?" she stammered.

Shane closed the bathroom door. He walked over to the side of the tub and slipped to his knees. Raelynn saw his gaze sweep over her body once more. He stuck his index finger in the water and made a small circular gesture along the surface stirring the calm water to a gentle ripple. "You wanted to know about me. Ask me a question. I'll answer." Shane said.

"Did you rob the bank?" she asked.

"No."

"Are you lying?"

He stared at her. She knew he was.

"What happened? Why did you leave and return for this?"

"My mother."

"I don't understand?"

"She enjoyed my success far more than I ever did. Drinking is her issue. Bad men too. All I can say is she got in some trouble. It took a lot to get her out of it, and I needed to leave Boston to clear my head. Once I lost the match against KB there was no reason to stay. So I left. My cousin found out where I was, told me he was in some trouble. I came back to help him. That's the truth. As close to the truth as anything I've said to you Rae."

"Your cousin was in trouble with Ian Higgins?"

"I didn't say that." His hand slipped into the water. Raelynn opened her mouth to object but when his palm touched her knee she forgot why she should. Instead she let go a deep sigh as his hand eased up her thigh, and water splashed a bit at the sides of the tub. "You are so beautiful Raelynn. That's the first thing I noticed. Your beauty."

"And the second thing?" she asked when his hand stopped at the apex of her sex. His gaze lifted. His hand slipped between her tightly pressed thighs and though she knew better, she parted her knees under his persuasion. His touch kindled feelings of fire she couldn't deny.

"Your balls." He winked.

Raelynn laughed. She shot upright sending a big wave of water over the side of the tub. Shane's shirt was soaked. Instead of him drawing back he slipped a finger inside of her tightness and captured her mouth at the same time.

Her eyes grew large in surprise but her tongue moved against his fully accepting the kiss. The caress of his lips over her mouth was electrifying. With extreme effort she pushed down the climax his thrusting finger almost drove her too, and enjoyed it's plundering. Her arms lifted around his neck and she pulled Shane half way into the tub as she reclined back. More water splashed, drenching Shane and spilling over to the floor.

Neither of them cared. She loved the way he kissed her. Which is why the cigarettes had to go. Thankfully she didn't taste ash and tobacco on his breath. Hot and heavy was his deep throat kiss and Raelynn let go of herself allowing passion to ride her close to the edge. He rewarded her submission by giving her another finger. The rush of pleasure that ensued when his thumb rubbed her clit was almost painful. "Oh yes!" she moaned then bit his bottom lip and drew it between her teeth. She groaned while Shane's wonderful mouth slipped from her lips and began to suck and lick at her neck with sensuous mastery. His lips seared a path down her throat to her shoulders

It was enough to make Raelynn cry out his name as he continued south, and his face submerged in the tepid bath water so he could capture her left nipple into his mouth. He teased it with light sucks and nips that forced her to grip the back of his head. Hell he could come all the way into the tub and she'd part her thighs and go for it. Her hips gyrated upward and her back arched. A wave of tingling heat spread from her clitoris to her channel as his two fingers thrust in and out of her slowly.

This shouldn't happen again. Stop it Raelynn. Don't make the same mistake twice.

"Mmm-ooo-re." She managed to stutter.

Shane's mouth rose from her breast and he kissed the side of her face, then pressed his lips against her ear while he spoke in a husky needy voice. "Let me have you, one final time. Say yes Rae."

"Yes." She said immediately, but soon winced at her weakness.

Shane pulled back, removing his hand as well. Raelynn shuddered visibly. She was so close. It was cruel to not finish her off. She flashed him an angry accusatory glare for making her body sing then ending the concert. But he had other intentions. With the strength of a Viking king he swooped her out of the tub into his arms. Raelynn gasped. More water came with her and out of the tub than stayed in. He held her to his chest as rivulets of bath water dripped from every inch of her.

"Get the door Rae," he grunted using the nickname only those closest to her did. Instead of talking herself out of it she reached out and turned the knob then pulled the door open. Shane brought the door fully open with his foot and carried her into the room. He decided against placing her on top of the neatly made bed, he set her down on her feet. Raelynn discovered she was short of breath. Her body pulsed with need.

Shane however, didn't seem to notice what a kiss and touch from him was doing to her. Instead he went back into the bathroom and retrieved a towel. Raelynn closed her eyes and tried to will her heart to stop pounding madly in her chest. It was ridiculous. She shouldn't be this excited about sex.

It soon dawned on her that the night was a bust. She didn't have condoms. She wouldn't dare sleep with him without them. Her eyes flashed open. Shane began to dry her shoulders.

"We don't um, have protection. This really isn't a good idea."

"I have something in my wallet." He said casually not acknowledging her doubts. His nonchalant manner was disarming. He sure was confident. She found his confidence sexy and infuriating. *Wait he has condoms?*

Raelynn's eyes narrowed into two suspicious slits. She lifted her arms as he continued to dry her off. She wanted to demand an explanation. After all they had just had sex yesterday, why would he be on the prowl so soon?

Instead she held her tongue. Especially when the pat down brought him to his knees before her and his face to her crotch. She stared down at the top of his head, partially wet from their playtime in the tub. He was still a mystery. One of the bad guys. Her hand trembled with nervous energy as it smoothed across and down the top of his head, careful of his stitches and bruises.

Last night had been different, an experiment. Now her eyes were open, and what she knew for certain was that Shane Lafferty's kisses and caresses were a gentle show of neediness from him. One that she ached to fulfill.

Raelynn let her fingers go through his silky strands and graze his scalp. The action caused Shane to stop with the drying, dropping the towel. He pushed his face into her sex, letting his palms glide up the backs of her thighs to cup both sides of her ass.

Lifting her left leg she draped it over his shoulder and he responded immediately giving her pussy a full on kiss. He teased her clitoris, with the tip of his tongue and let it trace between the folds of her sex then circle her opening before plunging in. Raelynn's head fell back and she instinctively gripped his hair tighter in her hand. Despite the balancing act she tried to maintain, she gyrated against his mouth wanting more.

His name escaped her lips in a wonderful chant that sang through the room. What he abandoned in the bathroom he was going to give her now in that moment, and it couldn't come a moment too soon. Once the delicious waves of pleasure coiled and tightened in her pelvis, she smashed her pussy into his face and dropped her head forward, taking in hard breaths.

Her entire body vibrated, and her cunt constricted. She tensed all over, climaxing on his tongue. The sudden release of her passion didn't stop, though her leg nearly gave out and she fell back on the bed. Shane went after her. He threw both her legs apart, making them fall on his shoulder, continuing to lick and suck her dry. Raelynn purred through a warm release, clutching the sheets in her hands.

Mmmm! Yes!

Almost reluctantly he drew away and forced himself to rise. Dazed and satisfied she managed to stare up at him as he shed his wet clothes. It was then she saw the bruising on his chest from the beating he suffered earlier. Her lustful quakes subsided and she rose on her elbows. "Shane stop. Wait." She panted. "Are you okay, I mean physically? An hour ago someone was pounding on you with a lead pipe."

"I've been hit harder, I'm fine."

"I'm serious. This doesn't have to happen, hell it shouldn't…"

"Rae. This will happen."

She bit down on her bottom lip.

His pants dropped. A meaty bobbing cock waved in greeting. Again Raelynn wondered who made up the lie that white men had small dicks. Many of her friends believed that crap. Shane proved the stereotype wrong.

"I'm not letting you out of this bed tonight," he said through clenched teeth. He picked up his wallet and opened the billfold. For her delight, he tossed four condoms on the bed. Raelynn snatched up the silver rectangular wrappers and relaxed. When Shane lowered and crawled to her she scooted back into the pillows until the headboard hindered her retreat. He covered her before she could verbalize her desires. His mouth claimed hers and she was lost in the pleasure it gave. Shane's tongue moved in decadent swirls and the tension in her body released once more. Gone were the aftershocks of her earlier explosion. She felt her racing heart stabilize.

The thick semi-erect shaft pressed between the lips of her pussy glided up and down her tender opening, arousing her again. Soon he was rock hard, and the pressure became more than she could take. Raelynn tore her mouth from his kiss and reached for the condoms, but his hand fell on top of hers, his fingers threaded between.

"Something you want to say Beautiful?" he said running his tongue over the small diamond stud in her lobe.

"I... stop teasing me."

He groaned, nipped her ear then lifted his face. She returned her gaze to his. She wouldn't beg for sex. If they were going to do it then they should do it. *Why was he prolonging this?* His fingertips touched her cheek. The gentle way he touched her sent a current of desire through her skin and he brushed his lips against hers very softly.

"What are you waiting for?" she asked breathlessly.

Shane lifted, and she scooted back toward the headboard. He snatched up the roll of condoms, and swiftly ripped into it before easing the ring over his swollen cockhead. She licked her lips in anticipation. They could play later.

At that very moment she wanted him inside her, rocking every thick inch of his cock in and out of her. He didn't wait for another invitation. Instead he fell on her body and the bed squeaked. She smiled, pleased. The heat from his strong form covered her completely. Shane ran his hand over and under her left thigh and lifted her leg, opening her. She pointed her foot north with a dancer toe to firm her calve and thigh for him. He seemed pleased as he pushed her leg further west and lifted it to angle his cock above her opening.

Anticipation swirled like an electric mist through her veins. She cupped her nipples and began to soothe their torment with her own pleasuring massage, her throat going dry, bracing for penetration. Raelynn's heart hammered in her chest and she began to roll her hips as each passing second felt like an eternity. Then he thrust downward and the thick invasion shattered the last of her self-control.

"Yes sexy," he said, his hot, moist breath brushed her ear as he sank deeper and covered her. "Soo, good," he groaned, slipping his hands underneath and squeezing then parting her butt cheeks to open her fully, allowing himself to get ball deep. Raelynn gripped his arms, throwing her hips upward in sync with his downward strokes. Every nerve ending along her clenching channel was on fire from the heated friction of his thrusting shaft. Raelynn could barely catch a breath between pumps. Her back arched off the bed and her nails cut into his flesh as she rocked with him. "Keep going, yes, yes, like that," she wheezed.

Shane withdrew all the way to the ring of his cockhead then shot his hips forward and gave her all seven inches, stretching her sweetly.

"Please! Please! Please!" she begged. Not sure for what.

He came down on her hard and pumped at her pussy with such intensity her toes curled towards the bottoms of her feet. A hard bite hit her shoulder and Raelynn cried out as he power drilled his cock into her taking them both to the brink. Her thoughts swam, and she shuddered hard in his arms joining in his climax.

Shane stayed on her. He kissed the bruising on her shoulder, and finally pulled out. He withdrew then rolled off her to his back. Rolling the condom from his dick he rose and went to the bathroom. She imagined he wanted to flush it down the toilet. Raelynn curled her body and held herself through the aftershocks of pleasure. Sex was so intense with him she felt as if her brain had shorted out. Already she was dreaming about the next round. They had four condoms after all.

Behind her she felt the mattress dip and his return. He drew the comforter they had kicked down to the edge of the bed over her and his body framed naturally to her curves. She smiled.

Soft tender kisses brushed her back and his strong arm eased around her.

"What are we doing Shane? We barely know each other."

"Let's think about it in the morning. We're here now. Why deny each other the pleasure?"

"True," she said around a yawn.

"True." He repeated, snuggling her.

Her lids slowly drifted asleep.

An hour, maybe two had slipped by. It wasn't even midnight yet, and already he craved her again. This babe was sexy as hell. Having her soft ripe ass pushed up against him wrecked his ability to reclaim sleep.

There was another reason however. His body was a train wreck. He thrived off of the rush he got from seducing and having Raelynn. The crash afterwards though left him dazed and winded. He couldn't decide if his head or his chest hurt more. Shane waited a few minutes to own his discomfort. He wasn't a pain junkie, but he'd weathered far worse and landed on his feet.

He lifted his wrist and confirmed that it was only 10:30. She stirred but didn't wake. So he rested the uninjured side of his face in his palm and eased down the sheet from her shoulder to reveal her curves. He was right about her being sexy, and he noticed something more. She was gutsy, classy, a league ahead of the women he usually preferred in his bed. And her body inspired the selfish beast in him, made him want to forget all his aches and pains and beat his chest like Tarzan.

Then fuck her wild and uninhibited.

Raelynn's skin was smooth and even toned like melted caramel, no stretch marks or blemishes. She moved and he eased a bit so she could turn to him. His gaze lingered on her flat but large dark nipples. One look at those juicy tips and he felt heat warm his groin. Everything about her was turning him on. Even the perfume of her sex all over his cock and the sheets got him off. Shane eased down onto the pillow, now face to face with her.

Raelynn's lids were closed with a fan of dark lashes that rested on her cheekbones, and thin but silky brows arched perfectly. Her nose was a bit fuller around the nostrils, and her lips were thick, perfect for sucking. His gaze snagged on her lips.

Before he could talk himself out of it he pressed his to hers. He expected her to wake and push him away. Tell him it was wrong, that she wanted out of this crazy dance between them. Instead her arm lifted slowly and embraced him. Those plump lips of hers parted to invite his tongue in.

Shane groaned deep in his throat and rolled her sweet body under him. Raelynn parted her thighs. She raised her hips so that he could feel how wet and warm she was for him, on command. His cock twitched from the brief contact.

He was all raw emotion when he gave her an inch. Squeezing his eyes shut he shuddered with love over the soft sexy feel of her body underneath him. It forced him to bite down hard on the inside of his jaw from the restraint he summoned not to pound her pussy into oblivion. He gave her a little, and a little more before her clenching channel drew him so deep he cursed in celebration.

The beast in him roared, forcing his hips to move faster, and he thrust in and out of tight, wet, heat harder and harder. It got so good he punched the headboard above her head. Raelynn giggled, she wrapped her arms around his neck moving her sweet body like a Goddess beneath him. Nothing in his life was this good. Nothing.

His world narrowed down to this sexy moment, this pleasure. Keeping his hand flat to the headboard he used the other to scoop under her and forced her to lift an inch to angle them both right for the intense sensations coursing through their bodies. He continued to pound her pussy until they both slipped into an endless void of rhythmic jolts that rained undiluted satisfaction over them.

"Let me… get on… top," she pleaded. Shane hesitated. His chest was already tight with pain and tension. What a way to die, with her riding him to the brink. His threshold for pain notwithstanding, there was another threat. If she kept loving him this way he may never be able to let her go.

Shane blinked the sweat from his eyes and rolled them so she could ride his cock. Raelynn stretched upward and thrust her hips back and forth never breaking their rhythmic dance. He tried to focus but her moves made his eyes flutter and his jaw clench. She began to bounce on his dick, with her hair wild and in her face.

Her passionate thrusts sent spasms of pleasure and pain through his chest. He gripped her thighs in a desperate attempt for mercy. Raelynn arched backward grabbing his knees and bounced harder. He could see down the line of his body to the bottom of his shaft disappearing in her swollen pussy lips as she rose and fell. He began to convulse with the shakes of a pending orgasm.

"Damn baby," He heard himself stammer.

Raelynn came forward, bracing her hands to the headboard and rubbing those swollen tight nipples on his chest as she bounced her ass on his cock over and over. He smoothed the sweat down the sides of her chest then over her back. He bent his knees and scooted a bit to capture a dangling nipple and sucked on it, hard. Raelynn hissed but her moves didn't stop. She rode his dick hard and fast, racing toward the pleasure point he felt building between them. It became an impossible task to delay his orgasm a minute longer. Shane's couldn't breathe, his balls cramped for release.

"Rae, give me a break." He pleaded forcing her down to his chest by locking her to him with his arm over her back and his hand on her ass. He shot his hips up and nearly shouted into her ear as he exploded.

She collapsed in exhaustion. He did the same. They lay locked in a shared embrace as their bodies shook through each climatic wave going through them. Shane wasn't aware how long he had been in her. But when he felt her go soft, no longer rigid and tight with tension, her pussy softening around his shaft, he gently rolled her to her side, and threw his leg over her thigh.

Raelynn was beautiful. He swore he could lie there and hold her for eternity, just like this. She snuggled his chest and he groaned. He was in fucking trouble. Slowly she pulled off his dick then turned over to give him her backside. It hit him like a pail of cold water to the face. He didn't remember rolling on a condom pre-entry. Had he?

Shane reached under the covers and touched his dick. He discovered he hadn't. "Fuck!" he grunted.

"Something wrong?" she mumbled in her sleep.

"Ah, no, no I'm cool." He kissed her shoulder then quickly slipped from the bed. Shane grabbed the strand of condoms and headed to the bathroom. If she found out he went into her raw she'd probably flip. He didn't mean to do it. Things developed so naturally between them it just happened. But she wouldn't believe him. Fuck, he was such a stupid fucking idiot. She probably thought what was sticky between her legs was her own cream. "Damn, what the fuck am I going to do?" He mumbled.

"Shane?"

"Yeah. Yeah." He said ripping a condom pack from the strand and tossing the foil in the trash to cover his secret. It was wrong. He should tell her of his mistake. But something held him back. The devil on his shoulder whispered that secrets and lies was all that could keep a woman like her with him. He should enjoy her, all of her, and not let anything, even her doubts get in the way.

"Shane? Come back to bed."

He cut off the light and returned to bed. She immediately rolled up against him and snuggled his chest. "What took you so long? I like using you as my pillow," she purred.

"Yeah, I like it too." He smiled.

CHAPTER SEVEN

Raelynn woke to a tangle of arms and legs. Her lover's heavy body partially covered hers. He held her so tight to him she could feel the rhythmic beating of his heart through his chest into her back. His face pressed to the back of her neck, she could feel the soft puffs of air from his breathing brushing her skin. It sent little tickles down her spine. Raelynn smiled.

When she tried to move Shane clung even tighter to her, pressing his cock between the split of her butt cheeks. The coarse pubic hairs at the base of his shaft brushed against her bare ass sending sexy currents through her skin that made her clit swell and her pelvis fill with warmth.

This was a taste of heaven.

She moaned. There was a dull ache between her legs, the sweet remembrance of how his cock stretched her below and branded his territory. She hoped to carry that feeling of him with her for the rest of the day.

Raelynn opened her eyes. *Did she just think that? Was she really falling for sex and not the guy?* She tried to look back over her shoulder but his face was buried low. Part of her knew the truth. She was falling for the guy as well. Shane could have been so much more in life. But yet he chose the easy way out. That's all she had learned from the time they spent. When things got tough he got going, or worse, he got to stealing.

Anger boiled to the surface dissolving the giddy euphoria of new attraction. Her anger would be a good thing between them. It would make sure that she kept her heart under lock and key. Far from his reach.

Disappointed, but accepting of the truth over their fated union, she shrugged her way out of his arms. He reached for her but she shook off his touch and rose. It was three in the morning. She needed to wash his and her sex off. The drive back would cost her if she didn't leave in time to get home and changed.

Raelynn entered the bathroom and flipped the light switch. The entire room flooded with a blinding light that almost knocked her back out of the door. She squinted and turned to a shocking reflection of herself in the mirror. Her hair was atrocious. No comb or brush could tame the wildness. It was as thick as a lion's mane and as full as an Angela Davis afro. "Damn, damn it," she groaned.

The best she could hope for today was a ponytail clip until she could get to her place and try to press out the kinks. Raelynn frowned. She stepped closer to the mirror. There was a thatch of bruised skin, red swelling on her collarbone. "Oh hell, no." What she found was the primitive evidence of their night together. She would have to wear her blouse buttoned up to the collar and turtlenecks until all traces of it faded.

Raelynn shook her head in disgust. There would be no going back now. She might as well face the truth. Raelynn opened the glass shower door and reached inside to turn the large dial. Immediately a spray of cold water rained down on her making her yelp in surprise.

"What you doing?"

Raelynn spun toward his voice. Shane rubbed his jaw. The bruising to the left side of his face had swelled from underneath the bandage she used to cover his stitches. And the scrapes and bruises on his chest made her bite her lip in pity. How was he able to remain standing, let alone perform the sexy acrobatics he put on her in bed? In the dark room, caught up in passion, she didn't see his body this way. But now he stood naked, exposed, and vulnerable. "I was going to take a quick shower before we left."

"I'll join you," he said closing the bathroom door.

"Maybe that's not a good idea."

Shane flashed her a sheepish grin. He plucked the remaining condoms from the bathroom counter and waved them in front of her face. "But we got two left."

"I'm serious. Last night, it was the wine, the bump on your head, things got away from us. But you know this can't really go any further. Right? Do you?"

He walked over and kissed the top of her head, held open the shower door and stepped inside. Raelynn threw her hands up in defeat and joined him. Thankfully the spray had warmed considerably, and she moved over, sharing the small space with him.

The mutual attraction between them tinged the air. She felt compelled to touch him. He wordlessly acted on his urges by lathering his hands with a bar of soap then rubbing it over her shoulders and down her arms. The fresh lather sent a swirl of lemony fragrance into the air and cleared her head. His hands continued over her chest then down her stomach and around her hips. Raelynn resisted the urge to speak. Instead she ran her hands gently across his bruises hoping to ease him into comfort.

"I'm no fool Rae, I know last night was our finale. There is no future with us." He traced a finger down between the valley of her breasts and stopped at her navel. His eyes slowly lifted and met her stare. "You are my biggest temptation now."

"Mine too. I mean, yes, it was a one time thing." She had to look away.

"What I can do is make sure you understand that no matter what happens I won't do anything to hurt you. Look at me."

Her gaze returned to his.

"My life is shit. Not anyone's fault. I made bad choices. Got to live with them. You and I are meant to be on different sides. I get that. I won't say or do anything to the contrary. Do you understand me? After tonight, no matter what happens out there, we never met."

"Take my offer Shane. Let me help you. Things for you and your cousin don't have to end badly."

He returned to lathering and massaging her breasts. The feel of his hands moving over her nipples made them painfully tight. She stepped back, directly under the pour from the showerhead. She flinched instinctively when her hair was flattened to the sides of her face and water streamed into her eyes. Lifting her arms to his neck she drew his face again to hers. She kissed his chin. His lips slowly descended and met hers. The kiss he gave was as challenging as it was rewarding. She was caught up. Her consciousness seemed to ebb, then flame alert from the taste of him. Shane wrapped her up in his arms in a crushing display of ownership. Blood pounded in her brain, leapt from her heart, and made her knees tremble. She was lost, completely under his spell once more. The kiss ended naturally.

"Let's finish bathing you," he said in a hoarse, dry voice.

He turned her to the shower wall and lathered every inch of her. Raelynn eagerly did the same when he was done. She paid special attention to his cock until she stroked it awake.

"Condom?" she asked.

He nodded. Reaching over to the soap dish and ripping into a silver packet. She took the slippery ring of the rubber and eased the cap over the head of his cock. Shane turned her to face the wall and pressed her to him. His hand cupped her left breast. He rolled his hips so his gloved dick could rub up and down the crease of her ass. Raelynn parted her feet and braced her hands to the tiled wall.

While he fondled her clit, he slipped his cock into her clenching pussy with slow methodical thrusts that sent her emotions into distress. Her lids fluttered shut as she was warmed from her hips to below from his thick entry. Soon he was pumping her pussy from behind and she was enjoying each strike. Rising on her toes and keeping the position she moved back against his invading cock taking him to the hilt. His hands slid down from her breasts to her belly and he kept her steady as he continued with his thrusts.

"Yes!" he grunted.

Raelynn bit down on her bottom lip and kept moving her ass in circular motions. Inch after inch came and went as he power drilled his passion for her until she reached her breaking point. He was bent over on her, his face slamming into the side of hers as he kissed her cheek, and then whispered his love for each part of her body in a thick lustful tone into her ear. Shane pinched her clit after each thrust and she creamed herself. Raelynn cried out gloriously. He pulled her back and she relaxed against him. He continued to lift her against his chest so she could ride his dick while locked in his embrace. If this wasn't ecstasy she didn't know what it was.

**

Kevin Reyes's eyes fluttered shut. The phone on his dash buzzed and he startled awake. Rubbing his eyes he looked at the time on the dash. He had to keep the car idling on and off so he didn't freeze his balls off in the cold.

"Uh, hello?"

"Agent Reyes?"

"Um, yeah, ah yes. Director."

"Anything to report?"

Reyes's gaze lifted to the small carpenter style home. The lights were off to the front of the house. Agent Traylor and their suspect hadn't emerged since they arrived. "No, not yet."

"You two will make that flight to Atlanta in the morning, after your visit with Rock Lafferty I want you to bring her to me."

"I understand." He ended the call. Kevin shook his head. Raelynn Traylor was a bright agent, from what he read. Why the hell would she risk her career and freedom helping a scumbag like Shane Lafferty? "A fucking waste." He grumbled slouching down and closing his eyes. He had nothing to do but wait.

Salvation
Volume III

CHAPTER EIGHT

"Rough night Agent?"

Raelynn Traylor reclined in the seat despite the request from the flight attendant that she not do so until they cleared take off. She arrived fifteen minutes late to the airfield. Her new partner's attempt to cover his annoyance failed. The scowl he wore caused his brows to lower over piercing eyes. Raelynn ignored him.

After Raelynn drove Shane home she had to hurry to her place and change. She then furthered the delay when she tried to tame her frizzy hair. Time spent in the shower making love with Shane left her with no choice but to smooth her unruly locks into a conservative chignon. She wore her standard blue pantsuit with a pressed white button down shirt. The lens of her sunglasses shielded her red swollen eyes. She took another sip of her coffee and swallowed before she addressed Kevin. "I'm fine."

Kevin shifted in the seat directly across from her. She met his stare. Something in his dark chocolate brown eyes irked her.

"Good to hear. We have a long day." A charming smile eased

across his lips. The man indeed had some good qualities. His skin was a deep brown, and his brows were dark and silky like the mustache over his top lip. His cologne was a strong citrusy fragrance that cleared her nasal passages. "Maybe we should debrief?"

"Debrief?" she stammered. "You have something else?"

Kevin's brow raised in surprise to her question. Of course she knew their orders. They'd meet with Calvin 'Rock' Lafferty and get needed information on Ian Higgins, or at best, his foot soldiers. What she didn't know was exactly how they planned to convince a lifer to turn his own son in.

Kevin used an electronic tablet on his lap to swipe through documents. He spoke while the plane taxied down the runway. "Calvin Lafferty known as Rock, let's see, he was convicted of double homicide in 1996. And… they suspect him for at least sixteen unsolved murders."

"Sixteen?" Raelynn shifted forward in her seat, alert. She sounded like a parrot. She needed to straighten up.

Kevin's gaze lifted then locked on her. "Maybe more."

"A hitman?"

"An enforcer. The men he killed were part of the Askovitch Crime family. Lithuanians tried to muscle in on territory near Dorchester Bay, Ian Higgins's territory in Southie. He got tagged because of the security cameras installed across the street of a… um, Douglas Junkyard. The victims were shot in the back of their heads execution style. When offered a deal Rock, clammed up. He pled guilty and went straight to sentencing."

"Ian Higgins must have a strong hold over him," Raelynn said.

Kevin shrugged. "Two murders are better than sixteen. He knew there was no deal that wouldn't land him in the penitentiary for the rest of his life. So why cooperate?"

"True." Raelynn nodded. "Maybe there's another reason why Lafferty didn't flip on Ian Higgins?"

"Like?" Kevin asked.

"I dunno. Not sure, just a feeling I have." Her throat dry, her palms clammy with sweat, she looked away. Raelynn tried to breathe through her anxiety but her lack of sleep made it hard. She prayed Kevin didn't notice. He appeared more fascinated with the story of Shane's father.

"To keep Rock from Higgins's reach we sent him to Atlanta where he's been ever since. Case closed."

The idea that this man raised Shane made her heart swell with pity. He sounded like a real piece of work. "Any contact between Rock and his son?"

Kevin shut the leather flap on the tablet. He wore a smug smirk on his face, an unflattering look of superiority Raelynn instantly disliked. "Nope. Doesn't mean he's not. In prison he's part of the Irish gang I.T.Z."

"A network of thugs that date all the way back to the Fire Kings, one of Chicago's first gangs during the antebellum," Raelynn said.

Kevin sat up straight. His eyes registered shock but he didn't voice it. Raelynn narrowed her gaze on him. "Yes, I know all about ITZ, I'm part of Homeland Defense remember? We monitor the gang activity of those with international ties. ITZ, Fire Kings, all of them trace back to Ireland."

"True. So you understand that they don't take kindly to non-Irish, especially us of a darker hue."

Raelynn rolled her eyes. What Kevin meant was that these men were white supremacists and Irish loyalists. She knew Ian Higgins had supremacist views but she didn't believe it true of Shane. She touched his heart, and no matter how badly scarred he was on the surface; he had a caring soul. It reached beyond color lines.

Are you sure Raelynn? After all you only slept with the guy, that doesn't make him some wounded misunderstood hero.

"So why are they sending in two black agents to deal with this man?" Raelynn silenced the voice in her head and focused.

"He will reject us, I'm sure, but we'll get his attention. My Director wants him angry, and if we can tap into that emotion—"

"We can unnerve him enough to gain something useful?" Raelynn finished the thought for Kevin. "We go in and tell him Shane... um his son, is in trouble I suppose? That we're after his boy, and he'll want to stop us? Give us something useful on Ian Higgins?"

Kevin nodded.

Raelynn licked her lips and asked the next question carefully. "Um, how do we know that... um, that Shane Lafferty is part of this bank robbery? The informant could be feeding us false information. Any, um, physical evidence?"

Kevin stared at her. He didn't answer.

Raelynn removed her sunglasses. "Problem with my question Agent?"

"You're a smart girl Raelynn..."

"Girl?" Raelynn frowned.

"Excuse me, woman, I think you and I both know that we can only trust these men to be self-serving bigots. All of them. The informant is as guilty as Shane Lafferty and Ian Higgins. We are just here to help them slit each other's throats."

Raelynn reached her limit. "You're right. I am smart, not book smart Agent, people smart. The first thing they taught us at Quantico is to see people for who they are, history, environment, and religious beliefs included. The second thing is that you understand who he wants you to presume him to be. I don't think we have to slit throats to get these men. We just need to understand their motivation and use it to our advantage—by the letter of the law."

Kevin smirked but didn't disagree. She looked away from his unwavering stare and focused on the clouds the aircraft sailed through. Her mind flashed to the conversation she had with Shane before their final goodbye. Did she believe what she just said? Even now she had no clue who Shane Lafferty really was.

"I guess this is it." Shane mumbled.

Raelynn's gaze slipped over and her vision focused on his shadowy profile. Very little light seeped in the car from the passenger windows. Still she ached with sympathy over the sight of the bruising to the side of his face, and the shared disappointment in his voice over their parting. He wore a baseball cap with the bib turned to the back of his head covering his dark locks of hair. He stared at his apartment building and made no move to open the door.

Would the night of passion she shared with him end here? It had to, she told herself. Even now he refused to discuss the trouble with Ian Higgins. Raelynn didn't know if she could help him even if he did come clean. The facts were clear.

Shane either robbed the bank, or had something to do with the robbery. He was in too deep.

Did she like him? Yes. Did she enjoy the passionate sex they shared? Yes. Did she want to see him again, take him home to meet her family, make him her main guy? No. This would definitely be the end. The next time she saw Shane Lafferty she would likely be placing him in handcuffs.

"I wish you'd consider my help. I know you're in something deep. I can only promise you it will get worse."

Shane reached for her. Raelynn moved her face and avoided his touch. Blood pounded in her brain, leapt from her heart, and made her hands tremble with the need to return his affection. So she gripped both hands tightly to the steering wheel for control. "Please go Shane."

He hesitated and she looked over just in time to receive his kiss. At first she thought to pull away, but the sample of his tongue and the feel of his mouth covering hers weakened her resistance. Her emotions whirled and skidded over the implications of her behavior. The grip to the steering wheel loosened. Raelynn touched his face gently; careful of his bruising she deepened the kiss. His hand unbuttoned the top of her blouse, his fingers were icy but his palm was fiery hot when it slipped inside to cup her breast and squeeze. Shivers of delight followed once his tongue swept in and flicked at the roof of her mouth, and the kiss hurled them toward another and another. She remained shocked by her own eager response to his passion for her, and did little to resist. Raelynn leaned forward and enjoyed the pinch to her tightly swollen nipple. Why did he have to be Shane Lafferty?

Why not some mechanic, or schoolteacher, a regular guy she could enjoy for as long as the flames of desire burned between them?

Shane stopped. Nose to nose he panted for breath and so did she. Then he took her mouth with savage mastery, shocking the air from her lungs. Raelynn had been forced back into the door with the seatbelt as the only barrier between them. She grabbed his leather jacket and held on. Damn his lips were warm and sweet over hers. She'd never been so aroused from a kiss. The inner folds of her sex grew moist and swollen with need.

"Stop!" she tore her mouth from his.

Shane finally withdrew, and the pain over her rejection made his face flush and his eyes narrow angrily. But it soon passed. In his eyes she found understanding and a hint of sad resolve.

"Nice knowing you beautiful." He reached for the door.

Raelynn grabbed his arm. "Please. Let me try to help you."

"You have Rae. More than you can ever know. Don't come to the gym, don't come around here, and don't get in Ian Higgins's way. You see me Rae you go the other way, unless you coming for me for other reasons. Okay?"

She sighed. "Then this is bye."

"Right. Bye." He mumbled and got out. He opened the back door snatched up his gym bag and tossed it shut. He never looked back at the car. Instead long legs bounded up the steps to his apartment building. She rubbed her lips, now pouty and swollen from his kiss.

"Bye Shane."

"Traylor?" Kevin said, and she came out of her thoughts.

"Yes?"

"Phone?" he handed her his cellular.

Raelynn sat up and pressed the phone to her ear. "Agent Raelynn Traylor."

"Hello Raelynn, it's Melissa Harvey."

"Director, um yes, good morning." Raelynn's line of vision

shifted to Kevin who watched her closely. Melissa Harvey was the Director of the ATF and was leading the task force assigned to the Higgins case. She was also Kevin Reyes's boss.

"I'm told you and Agent Reyes are headed to Atlanta to meet with Lafferty?"

"Yes ma'am."

"Well, as soon as you return I want to see you in my office. Are we clear?"

"Um, okay, yes ma'am. Clear."

The line disconnected.

"Anything wrong?" Kevin asked.

Raelynn masked her worry with a blank expression. "No. Everything's fine. A debrief with your boss is all."

Kevin nodded. "Okay."

**

"Mom, wake up. Wake up dammit!" Shane tossed another empty Budweiser into the plastic trash bag from the collection of bottles strewn over the floor. His mother groaned. She opened her eyes then shut them again. He shook his head and collected the evidence from her night bender. She had her dry moments, but something would always set her back. Since his return she'd had blackouts. And he knew why, guilt.

"Get in the shower, you have to go to work don't you?"

"Can't today, don't feel good." She gurgled, rising to a sitting position.

"No shit! If you weren't drinking all night you wouldn't be sick now."

"Hey!" Margene shouted, and then touched her head, swaying a bit. Her blonde hair was stringy and matted to her head, and her eyes were swollen with dark puffy pockets underneath. She opened them and glared at her son. "Don't fucking curse at me. I'm your mother. Show some gat damn respect Shane!"

She struggled then rose from the sofa. Shane watched her stagger to the hall and disappear in search of her room. He heaved a deep sigh and bit back the snarky comment burning the tip of his tongue.

Margene had been a horrible mother, and years of her self-loathing had made her nothing but a sad burden. Though he despised her ways, as her son he could never truly abandon her. When he left two years ago, he always stayed in contact and sent money home. He should have cut all ties with South Boston. He understood that now.

Shane sat on the sofa. His head hurt, and so did his chest. A smile formed and he sighed. No matter how fucked up his life was he still had the feeling of Raelynn with him. The feeling of possessing a woman you knew was forbidden. The secret triumph of knowing she felt it too. And Raelynn did feel it. Shane closed his eyes and remembered their last time together.

The shower ended too soon.

Shane braced his back against the damp tile wall. He tried to capture air into his burning lungs. Never in his life had he felt so overwhelmed after sex with a woman. He might have really overdone it with his brown beauty this time. Every muscle and tendon in his body ached. It hurt to blink. Still he had to have her one last time. He could die a happy man between those soft thick thighs of hers. And if his dick wasn't a flaccid limp noodle he'd try her again.

Raelynn bent forward, only briefly, and turned off the running water. His cock twitched over the sight of her round perfectly shaped ass, slick and glistening with tiny pearls of moisture from the shower play. Instinctively his hand ran smoothly over her backside and he stroked his cock wishing it would revive. She straightened, her head turned and she smiled sweetly at him. "That was, um, good. I... I guess we need to get dressed now huh?" She said in a shy voice so foreign to the kick ass, ball-busting attitude she wielded when she wanted to squeeze him for information.

Did she feel it too? She looked away and exited the shower.

Yeah, she felt it too. Shane stepped out of the shower and his foot touched the disposed condom. His mind flashed back to the sex they shared in bed. The memory of his lapse of judgment when his common sense escaped him and he forgot to cover his cock before he took her burned his cheeks with shame. Raelynn didn't know, and that omission of the truth felt like a huge betrayal. Maybe he should tell her about the slip?

He looked up and she had already begun to dry those beautiful curves of hers. She denied him the pleasure. Their eyes met, reflected on the surface of the condensed mirror and she smiled for him again.

No. He couldn't tell her. She'd think he did it on purpose. It would give her another reason to hate him. Besides he tested clean. To box he had all kinds of physicals and his body was fit, except for his smoking habit. He had no doubt she tested clean too. Hell for all he knew she could be on the pill. No harm, no foul.

"Are you okay Shane? Something wrong?" she turned from the sink. Using the towel she covered most of her nudity, but those curvy hips of hers remained on display. Her hair had frizzed at the root and lay limp to her shoulders, wet on the tips, and her eyes glittered with merriment. She didn't look just beautiful but happy. Like some exotic being from a land far away from the bullshit kingdom he served.

"I'm okay." He said coming out of the shower stiffly. His cock still wouldn't respond but his desire for her had his heart beating hard and fast in his chest. He touched her chin, tilted it upward to draw her lips to his. She tasted so sweet. With his free hand he tugged the towel from her and she fought feebly to hold on to it. Eventually it dropped and cascaded to her feet.

"Shane, don't… we can't." Raelynn's voice came across breathy.

He stepped back and looked at her body under the bathroom lights. He loved running his hands over her voluptuous curves. Even now the swollen peaks of her dark berry nipples made his limbs tighten with anxious energy, and his mouth water for a suck. And he was supposed to turn away? Walk away and never look back? Fuck that.

Shane stepped to her pressing her back into the vanity. Her hands dropped to her sides for balance, her breasts heaved upward and she leaned backward. "I'm not done with you."

She laughed in his face. "Your cock says differently." She teased, lowering her eyes to his limp member pressed between the folds of her sex. Shane's face flushed. He groaned deep in his throat. His gaze lifted from where they touched intimately to her breasts once more. Her uneasy breaths made her nipples quiver. Shane licked his lips. Fuck his cock. There were many other ways to have her.

"Turn around woman and assume the position."

"Or what?"

"Or I'll use reasonable force." He warned, while desire formed a hard knot in his belly.

"Oooh, Shane the bad boy, had been wondering where you've been hiding him." She chuckled. He arched one brow. He had to wonder what scared Raelynn, certainly not the danger she'd placed her career and life in by associating with him. She must of read his thoughts. She leaned forward and rubbed her nipples over his chest. Her hand went to his side and stroked his hip. "You've given me a wonderful night. I won't forget it. But you're tired. I'm tired, and this has to end."

"I know." He admitted. "Give me a bit more and I'll accept it."

"But?"

"Turn around Rae."

"I told you my name is Raelynn."

"To me babe, you're Rae. Turn around."

Raelynn pushed him back lightly with both hands then turned and faced the mirror.

"Assume the position. I'm sure they taught you how in F.B.I. school." Shane chuckled.

"I'm sure they taught you how at county." She shot back.

Shane winced. "Owe, damn babe, you trying to wound a man?" he touched his chest. Raelynn smiled. She put her hands flat to the vanity countertop and spread her feet. Leaning forward over the sink her beautiful tits bounced and swayed a bit. Shane's gaze lowered to her backside. He looked down to his cock hoping it had awoken. And though he felt heat building from his balls and spreading through his shaft his weakened state gave him nothing more. The disappointment he felt didn't overshadow his desire. He ran his hand down her lovely spine and then cupped both halves of her round ass.

Slow and careful Shane lowered to his knees.

While Raelynn remained rigid, he relaxed. From his view her lovely pussy lips appeared swollen with desire, he parted the dark folds to see all of her pink perfection glistening wet. Shane understood what they shared bordered on animalistic, intense attraction. She would give him what he wanted, because her cunt swelled with the same urgent need. She smelled of soap and a heady tinge of arousal.

To inhale her made his heart beat faster.

He leaned forward and flicked his tongue at her clitoris coaxing the plump bud out on his tongue. He took a sexy sip and drew it between his lips. Passion for her consumed him and he gripped her thighs for strength. Raelynn lifted on her toes, putting a dip into her back with her knees parted, to offer herself for his eager mouth. Fierce, hot elation swept through him. He released her clit and slipped his tongue between her folds to reacquaint himself with her salty flavor.

Damn she tasted good.

He sat back on his haunches allowing his tongue to love her. It swept from the quivering hole of her pussy to her forbidden zone. Her arousal rose into his nostrils and he growled deep in his throat wanting to fuck her bad.

"Turn around Raelynn," he ordered, drawing away. Her legs visibly trembled. She managed to turn and sit on the edge of the sink. She grabbed his hair and lifted her left leg to rest her foot on his shoulder. Her jewel opened for him once more and he dove in. His tongue dipped into her clenched channel and she gasped loudly. He fucked her with his mouth, thrusting his tongue as deep as it would reach and then swiping it out and around her pretty tight hole. He clasped on her clitoris and gave her two fingers. She cried out again. His scalp burned. She gripped his hair so tight. Nothing stopped his passion for her.

Her breath hissed like a deflating balloon between parted pouty lips and another quiver travelled down from her heaving chest to her pussy. He could feel her trembling against his lips, and he drove her closer and closer to the final climax between them.

CHAPTER NINE

A fist beat hard against the wood door sending a thundering noise through the apartment. Shane shot upright on the sofa. He could still feel the disappointment burn his chest when he had to let Raelynn go. The euphoria over the memory of her submission faded fast. He narrowed his gaze on the door. The pounding sounded like one of authority and for a brief moment he imagined his brown dove with other federal agents ready to charge in and arrest him. The moment passed.

More knocking…

The time read fifteen past the hour. No one but Scotty would dare show up at such an early hour. A bit exhausted from his night with Raelynn, he tossed the bag of beer bottles and stiffly walked to the door. The pain wasn't centered in his skull or the side of his face any longer. Shane released the lock and opened the door. Standing before him was Ian Higgins and his right hand man, Big Al.

"What do you need?" Shane grumbled.

Ian's brow lifted to the gruff greeting. With a deep sigh of resolve Shane stepped back and allowed him to enter. Big Al glowered at Shane. His tall frame bowed to enter the door behind his boss. Yesterday while in Cambridge with Raelynn he called Scotty to find out if word on the fight with Mickey and Danny had hit the streets. Scotty said it had. Which meant Ian knew of it. A personal visit by the man only spelled trouble.

When he turned he watched in silence as Ian made himself at home by sitting at his mother's small dinette table. Big Al chose to stand against the wall with his hands tucked in to his leather pockets.

"You look like shit. Rough night?" Ian asked in a dull, unconcerned voice.

Shane didn't hear his mother to the back of the apartment. He prayed she had collapsed on the bed and was out cold again. He was in no mood to see Margene's reaction to Ian Higgins in her living room.

"I'm fine."

"Fine?" Ian chuckled deep in his throat. He removed his dark gloves and placed them on his lap, and then crossed his legs. "It's not how I hear it. Look at your face. You telling me you got that nasty shiner from a sparring match at Gladiators?"

"What did you hear exactly? What am I answering to?"

Ian Higgins scoffed, then glared.

Shane sighed. He stepped forward. "Mickey and Danny came at me in the alley behind Gladiators. They got the best of me. End of story."

Ian lifted a single finger for silence. Shane resisted the urge to lunge for the gun tucked in the cereal box in the kitchen and unload on them both. He loathed these men, hated everything about his life under Ian Higgins's control.

"Who is she? And Shane, don't lie to me. I won't tolerate it."

"Some babe I met in a bar two days ago. I fucked her and she came around the gym looking to hook up again."

"You fucking black women who carry guns?"

Shane swallowed his first response and thought of his words. "She's a little tough. Not sure who she works for. I think the gun is just something she has to protect herself. I got the feeling she's straight. She just appeared in the alley and drew on them. Fact is she saved my life. Then we crashed in Cambridge before she brought me home."

Shane knew telling the truth or a close version of the truth would be the only way to keep Ian off of Raelynn's scent. If the mob boss even suspected Raelynn as a federal agent he'd kill her. He waited for Ian to respond. It was a tense ten seconds of silence. Finally what looked almost close to a smile spread over Ian's face extending the grotesque scar that ran from his mouth to his ear. "Sounds like a bitch I want to meet. Wonder if she's with Tony Edwards's organization?"

"I can check into it boss." Al leveled his hard gaze on Shane. "What's her name Shaney?"

Shane dropped his head and shook it. "No fucking way. Look I'm in, I got no choice but to be in, you made sure of that. But you won't crawl through my personal life. To hell with that. The broad saved my life. I'm not going to bring her any heat by putting you on her."

Big Al stepped forward. He was a good six inches taller than Shane. "Give me her fucking name Shaney!"

"Wait a minute Al," Ian said. "Shane has a point. He can fuck whomever he chooses. I prefer my Irish beauties, but if he wants to dip between chocolate thighs I can give a shit. I'm not the bigot they say I am. We evolve. Is that what it is Shane? You've evolved? Looking to integrate Southie?" Ian rose with a deep chuckle. "This thing with you, Mickey, and Danny, I want it done. No more of this shit."

"They came after me." Shane grumbled, his fist clenched so tight his wrist burned.

"I understand, and it will be addressed. But that's the end." He leveled a finger at Shane. "I don't need you getting bad press so close to the fight. You know my wishes…"

"Shane? Who was at the door?"

Shane turned his head and Ian's gaze lifted as his mom stepped out of the hall. Freshly showered, the color had returned to her cheeks and her hair was slicked backward. She froze in shock then horror to see who their uninvited guests were.

"What the hell are you doing in here?" A sharp screech came from his mother as Margene marched out with her ratty pink robe buttoned up to the collar. "What are you doing in my damn apartment?"

"Hello to you too Margene," Ian said calmly.

"Shane?" Margene looked at him alarmed.

"It's cool mom. Calm down."

"Get out! Get out now!" she yelled.

Ian narrowed his eyes on Margene. He took a step toward her and she stepped back. Shane got between him and his mother. His nostrils flared. Every bone in his body tensed to protect her. He looked the evil dictator who had been a part of their lives since he was a kid in the face. "We done?" he asked.

Ian smirked, giving Shane a look over. "For now Shane. You do as you are told."

"Get out!" Margene yelled from over Shane's shoulder.

Ian winked at his mother then turned and walked out. Big Al followed.

Margene shoved Shane in the back and he winced stumbling forward. The pain cut him in his gut and sliced up to his throat. He whirled on his mother. "Calm down."

"No!" she said through fresh tears streaming down her cheeks. "I don't want him near us, or you. Not anymore Shane. No more of Ian Higgins dammit!"

"It's fine."

"It's never fine! Not when Ian comes around." She began to pace, visibly shaken. Shane sighed; he headed to the chair that Ian had vacated. His mother's past with Higgins had driven her to the bottle, and cursed Shane to a life of shit. He was too damn tired of the bullshit to care anymore.

"I'm sorry Shane. Okay? Forgive me, please. It was my fault that night. I got behind the wheel of the car. I hit that woman, ruined her life. You shouldn't have to pay for this mistake over and over again."

"Let it go mom."

"No! I ruined your life. You used Ian Higgins to cover up my crime. He used your guilt to make you foolishly believe you had to. I understand why you did it, took the blame for it, to keep me out of jail. Then you had to lose your fight, your career. You were right to leave Boston Shane, to leave all of us behind. Why did you come back here?

For him?"

Shane didn't answer. Margene wailed. "It's my fault," she pressed her hands to her head. "My fault, my fault, my fault."

"STOP!" Shane yelled at her.

His mother silenced.

"It's done. I'm back to box. Just to box. I'm not into anything with Ian Higgins. Okay?"

"I don't believe you. That man used your father until his heart dried up and he became as evil as he is. Turned him into a murderer. He can't have you too! Cass said…"

"Cass?" Shane glowered. If his mother had gone again to his mentor and trainer about him after all the damage she'd done, he'd kill her. Cass already stated his concerns. He needed them all to back off. Margene bit down on her bottom lip and swallowed the rest of her statement.

"Don't blame Higgins for Dad, Mom. Dad screwed things up all on his own."

"What do you know about it?" Margene shot back.

"I know you slept with Ian Higgins behind his back so what does that make you?"

Margene put her hand to her mouth. She stared at him with red-rimmed weepy eyes. "I made mistakes, your Dad and I both made mistakes Shane. But you're a man now. You're twenty-six for Christ's sake. You don't have to pay for my mistakes anymore. No more. Just go. Forget the boxing, forget Southie, and forget us all. Just get the hell out of here."

She turned and fled to her bedroom. Shane slumped forward.

He closed his eyes. For a brief moment with Raelynn he had a chance to forget how much he hated his life. Now he had no choice but to remember.

**

The buzzer sounded off and the door locks disengaged.

Raelynn sat up straight in her chair. Kevin stood behind her. Why he chose to take on the bad cop role confused her. The interview would be tense enough. She didn't question him. She had been wound tight with anxiety over this meeting. The warden escorted them personally to a room with four grey walls of concrete. The table before her was a standard card size table with fold out chairs. After a fifteen minute wait the prisoner was escorted in.

Rock Lafferty had to be at best six-foot-six or seven and four hundred pounds of solid muscle. He had a shaven head with a large shamrock tattooed over the top. The rest of his visible skin, except his face, had been covered in tattoos as well. His neck and arms outside of his short sleeves were inked up. He shuffled inside in an orange jumper with shackles on his feet and wrists. Three guards had to bring him in. Raelynn had little doubt a chained Rock Lafferty could snap all of their necks if he wanted to.

The inmate's eyes glowered and fastened on Kevin first. He paused when his gaze switched to her. Blue, and clear, Rock had eyes just like Shane. The hatred reflected there ended any comparison she would make. The man's sapphire blue, bottomless glare was nearly murderous. The shadow of contempt lurking in its depths made it hard to maintain her composure. There were people who belonged behind bars, and she knew Rock Lafferty was at the top of that list.

"Sit!" A guard barked.

Rock Lafferty shuffled to the seat. Raelynn wonder if the small fold out chair could hold his weight. He sat and it did.

"Hello Mr. Lafferty, my name is Agent Raelynn Traylor. Behind me is Agent Kevin Reyes."

Lafferty never tore his gaze from her face. He licked his lips, the way Shane did when he wanted something from her.

Stop it Raelynn, stop thinking of Shane. Deal with the animal before you and get your ass back to Boston.

"The feds know better than to send *your* kind to squeeze me. What the fuck are you doing here?" Rock asked.

Raelynn smiled. She ignored the reference to her 'kind' and thankfully so did Kevin. She opened the folder before her and removed a picture of Shane. She set it flat on the table. Rock Lafferty's hard gaze lowered to the image of his son. He said nothing.

"He's your son correct? Shane Lafferty a two time contender for a heavy weight championship?"

Rock Lafferty continued to stare at the image.

"I hear he was pretty good two years ago. What was his record Kevin?"

"6 and 0 until his bought with KB. Most think he took a dive." Kevin chuckled.

Raelynn nodded. She kept Rock Lafferty trained in her sight. "What do you think Kevin? Did Shane take a dive?"

Kevin stepped forward. "I saw the fight and I think KB, you know he's one of our kind, yeah, KB put him down because Lafferty had no rhythm."

Rock's hateful glare shot up to Kevin.

Raelynn cleared her throat. "Something happened two years ago. The fight went wrong for Shane, right? Now he's back, trying to reclaim his glory. You've heard of his return haven't you? Must make you proud."

Rock Lafferty didn't answer.

"He's in trouble, and you can help him," Raelynn said softly.

"Fuck him and you too!" Rock spat.

Raelynn flinched. Kevin put a hand to her shoulder as she struggled with how to respond. If Rock Lafferty didn't look like a meaner, bigger version of his son she might have known how too.

"Listen here Mr. Lafferty, Ian Higgins has your son in a tight spot—again. Now we know your life is shit, and will be shit until they throw you in the ground. We aren't here to offer you a deal, or even promise things can go easier for you."

Rock chuckled. "Boy, there's nothing I want from you that a white man won't come in after you and offer. So cut the shit."

Kevin stepped closer to the table. "That's just it Rock. The white man sent me, because no one cares if you rot in here. In fact they sent us both on this errand to keep us busy. You've been out of the circuit for quite some time. There are other players now, white, black, yellow, as long as the money is green everybody's in. Have you heard of the re-gentrification going through your old neighborhoods?"

"Ian Higgins knows what it is." Rock scoffed.

"Ian Higgins huh?" Raelynn cut in. She grew tired of the pissing match between the men. She needed something useful. "What exactly has loyalty to Ian Higgins done for you? You got the murder rap and Ian Higgins got your life. From the way I hear it you weren't just his enforcer; you were much more, weren't you? The two of you had big plans for Dorchester Bay. That's why you settled for prison, to keep your cause moving, and keep Ian Higgins in power. And what has that sacrifice done for Shane?"

Kevin frowned. She felt him withdraw from her side. Rock looked at her with renewed interest. Raelynn's gamble proved right. Kevin's method came across as too textbook. Well Raelynn decided to go off her instinct. A man as menacing and deadly as Rock Lafferty wouldn't go to jail for murder if he didn't have bigger secrets. Her guess was Ian Higgins didn't run Rock Lafferty as many believed. The gleam of interest in Rock's eyes said she could be right.

"Ian Higgins betrayed you. A lot of time has passed. Do you know what has become of Shane? Of your wife? Is this really what you wanted? To have no control? Or would you like to send Higgins a long overdue message. From *our* kind?"

Rock returned his gaze to Raelynn. "Tell the boy next to you to shut the fuck up, and you and I can talk sweetheart."

Raelynn blinked over at Kevin.

Rock smiled. "It's the only conversation I'll have."

"Give us a minute Kevin. Please."

"I'll give you ten. I suggest you use it wisely." Kevin hissed at Rock Lafferty then walked out. The guards remained.

Rock sat back. "You know my kid?"

"Me? No. I don't know him, I'm just here to…"

"To help him or fuck him over, whatever it takes to give your sweet ass the notch you need to make the climb right? I've met several agents, all of them hungry to go after Ian Higgins, several of them coming down here to squeeze me for anything they can use."

"I can help Shane if that's what you want. But you got to tell me how. I will make sure my superiors go light on him."

"Bullshit." Rock leaned forward. "The only way to help Shane is for you to bring him to me. Tell him I said Higgins has a hundred and when he's done he'll have a hundred more. He'll know what that means. Arrange a meeting between me and my son and you'll have Ian Higgins." Rock Lafferty rose and all the guards tensed. He snapped his neck from left to right, turned and walked out. Raelynn finally found air enough in her lungs to breathe.

CHAPTER TEN

"What's the prognosis doc?" Cass asked. He removed his half smoked cigar from his fat jaw.

The doctor rolled down his sleeve and Shane reached for his shirt.

"No broken ribs, no real damage, though that bang to his head gives me concern. Any dizziness Shane? Vomiting? Has your vision been impaired in any way?"

"No. No. And no." Shane grumbled.

"So he can train?" Cass pressed for the diagnosis he wanted.

The doctor frowned. In fact he looked appalled by the mere suggestion. "I think he needs to take a week or two to heal before he steps in a boxing ring."

"No fucking way." Shane snapped. "I got the fight next week."

The doctor looked from Shane to Cass with alarm. "You need to heal son. You won't do yourself any favors by pushing your body further. I'll schedule you for a CAT scan next."

"Enough tests. I'm fine," Shane waved off the offer.

"Hold on Shane." Cass stepped to the doctor. "Give him a b-12 shot or something doc, and something a little strong for the pain. We'll come back tomorrow for the CAT scan. If you say it's no good then understood. But he's right he has to fight. Ian Higgins is backing him."

The doctor shook his head. "I'll send in the nurse to discharge you. A b-12 shot won't do anything to heal you faster. Rest is your only answer."

Alone, Cass, Shane's manager and friend, cleared his throat. "We need to talk."

"I can fight Cass. I'm good. I swear it. Give me the shot of Jack Daniels and I'll forgo the pain killers."

"Margene called before you arrived at the gym. She says things with Higgins are worse than you said?"

"She doesn't know what she's talking about."

"She's scared for you Shane."

Shane sat down on the exam table. He winced at the discomfort slicing through his abdomen. "Really? After all the shit she and the old man brought into my life she's scared for me? Too late, the fight goes down the way Higgins wants. After that…"

"After? There is no after if you take a dive. It's over. And don't disrespect your mother in front of me. I won't have it."

Shane groaned. "I'm done Cass. I'm done. There's heat on me now. Winning isn't an option. Hell maybe we should call the fight?"

Cass stared at him for a moment. "Higgins would never allow

it! He knows all of Southie is behind you and this comeback. Heat? What kind of heat? Are you in deeper trouble Shane? Tell me what is going on?"

Shane knew the score. Cass and most of the old neighborhood had on blinders to the evils of the man. "Higgins don't give a shit about Southie or tradition Cass. I remember my old man used to say something every time a man in the brotherhood was lost because of another. Give a man a hundred and he'll take a hundred more."

Cass looked away and silence filled the rom. Rock Lafferty believed in their community, or so he said. Ian Higgins believed in nothing. He wanted power, and once he was done taking everything from everyone, men like Cass would be left with nothing, all of what they had and what was familiar would be gone. "I'm done being a puppet for them. I'm done carrying the old man's burden, Scotty's burden, Margene's burden. I'm done. This is my final payment then I'm taking Mom and leaving Boston. Higgins can do whatever the fuck he wants after that."

"Are you going to throw the fight or walk away from it?"

Shane smirked. Cass rolled his eyes shaking his head.

"What does he have on you? How dangerous can this get?"

Shane had no intention of answering the question. Raelynn had been right. He deserved to be free, and with freedom came a price. He would go for it. However he had to.

**

The drive back to the office had been tense. Kevin did compliment her on cracking Rock Lafferty enough to give them a shot at obtaining more. He agreed pulling Shane in to turn on Lafferty would be the next logical step. Raelynn felt sick to her stomach over it. She sat in silence replaying every little moment she spent with him. It would take awhile before she could separate Shane the man she knew, from the man he apparently was.

Kevin parked. When they walked through the building her phone buzzed on her hip. She answered while going through the traditional security search. "Hello?"

"Hey. What's up girl? How are you?"

"Andrea?"

"Yeah, I went by the house, um… what you have a party last night? Drink my bottle of Chianti."

"I can explain…"

"No need. Want to do dinner tonight? Catch up?"

Raelynn stepped into the elevator. She smiled at the thought of a dinner where she could tell her friend of the last forty-eight hours. "Let me call you when my day wraps."

"Cool. Bye."

"Bye."

The elevator doors opened. Kevin touched her arm. "We're not getting off here."

Raelynn paused. She looked to the panel and saw he had pressed the 15th floor button. Kevin let go of her arm. "Oh, Director Harvey wants to meet. Right."

Kevin stared at her and she couldn't ignore the questions in his watchful gaze any longer. "What's your problem? All day you've been giving me the eye. Is there something you want to say to me?"

"Just wondering a little about you. Who you are, really? Where are you from?" he asked.

Now he wanted to make conversation? He barely said anything but work related questions since they met this morning. Raelynn imagined his smug disapproval was due to her inexperience compared to his years in the field. She'd had the issue before. Andy, her partner didn't give her much slack when they were first put on a task force together. Which was surprising because Andy was as green as she was. Shaking off the irritant she stepped out the elevator feeling confident. After all Rock Lafferty would only speak with her. Any break in the case with his help would indeed go to her credit. It looked like things were changing.

"Florida."

"Oh, love Florida," he smiled.

Raelynn opened her mouth to ask about him when she noticed several men approached. One in particular looked familiar. He glanced up at her and paused with the same sense of recognition. Then they passed through a door.

"Something wrong?"

"Who... who was that?" Raelynn stammered.

"Who was who?" Kevin asked concerned.

Oh shit! Raelynn remembered. It was the man wailing on Shane with a lead pipe in the alley. The same man she drew a gun on. Did he see her? Did he recognize her? What the hell was he doing here?

"Raelynn? You okay?"

"Yes. I'm fine."

"Director Harvey is waiting. Down the hall." He turned to

leave.

"You aren't coming?"

"We'll talk soon." He cast another smug look over his shoulder and kept going. Raelynn nervously ran her hands down her hips. She walked past the closed door. The thug was with agents. Could he be the informant? Damn it to hell did her superiors know? They couldn't have. The man looked equally surprised to see her. First things first, she needed to face the Director and make sure she clearly explained her intentions, her motivation, and her commitment to the bureau. Neutralize any threat this man would pose.

The door opened before she reached for it. Elliot Greaves stepped back and gave her a wan smile. Director Melissa Harvey of the ATF stood over near the window looking out at the city. She turned with the same blank look on her face.

"Agent Traylor, have a seat, please."

Raelynn did as ordered.

Melissa Harvey was a very attractive woman but she muted her beauty under her ironclad seriousness. "So I hear Rock Lafferty couldn't be of any help."

"No, um I mean yes ma'am. Though I have to tell you that we might be able to use him if we play things his way."

"His way?"

"He wants to see his son. I think an arranged meeting between the two of them could indeed turn them both to our side and at the very least force Ian Higgins's hand. We can make an offer…"

"Like the one you've made?" Director Harvey smirked.

"Excuse me?" Raelynn frowned.

Commander Greaves reached to the desk and picked up a folder, he handed it to Raelynn. This was the third time a folder of some sort had been placed in her hand. Each time her heart raced. She was still shaken from seeing the informant in the hall who could blow her cover. Now what could this be? She searched the faces of her superiors for an explanation. With no choice she opened it. The first image knocked the wind out of her chest. A zoomed lens photographed her in the car this morning kissing Shane. Raelynn shut the folder immediately. "I can explain."

The Director's brow winged up, and amusement danced in her eyes.

"I didn't know who he was…."

"Before or after you slept with him?" The Director asked.

"It started two days ago."

"Spare me Agent. Don't you think we already know when this started?"

Raelynn looked to her mentor and boss. Elliott Greaves met her stare with a cold one of disapproval. How could she have been so reckless? "I called you sir, yesterday and told you I was following up on a lead," Raelynn began.

Melissa Harvey rose. She crossed her arms in front of her and stared down at Raelynn "Don't worry agent, there's a way out of this mess. A way for you to salvage your career, and possibly get a promotion."

Raelynn double blinked.

Melissa nodded to Greaves. "We're sending you undercover."

"Undercover? He knows I'm an agent…"

"Exactly." Melissa said. "And we know he robbed that bank. We know that he's tied to Ian Higgins and his gun smuggling ring. We know that in three days he will throw a fight that will fund Ian's purchase from his contacts in Ireland for guns. The same guns he's trafficking to terrorists through his Lithuanian allies."

"So, if you know all of this why do you need me?" Raelynn asked.

Melissa walked away. She sat behind Elliot's desk and spoke calmly. "Because knowing and proving are two different things. I need evidence, the irrefutable kind. My informant says that Shane is going to take the dive. Make him believe you are torn over this unexplainable attraction you two share. Convince him that you will help him escape federal prosecution. Gain his trust the best way you can and we'll get him to wear a wire. Agent Reyes will be your shadow."

"Okay. So we're cutting him a deal.

"No deal Agent."

"Excuse me?"

"You heard me. No deal."

"Why? Shane's probably willing to come in, to work with you. I just need time. If we can give him immunity and witness protection then…"

"Not going to happen. We've already made that deal with his nemesis Mickey. You met him. The man you drew your weapon on in the alley?"

Raelynn felt sick.

"Melissa, it might be wise to hear her out." Her boss said. "Especially if we can convince him to speak with his father, we can solve many cases by helping Shane Lafferty. How is she to convince him to wear a wire without a deal?"

"Oh she'll do it. He trusts her," Melissa smirked evilly at Raelynn. "Aren't I right? You can make him all the sweet promises you need to, as long as we get him in that wire." Melissa narrowed her eyes on Raelynn. "You are sworn to uphold the law, not help criminals usurp it. Shane has others he wants to protect. Read the file agent. Then pay your boyfriend a visit."

"So you're saying I have to set him up."

Melissa smirked. "Either you do so or I'll make sure you never leave your desk again."

**

"Shane! Shane wait!" Scotty shouted. He dropped down on the seat of his motorcycle and looked back. His cousin shuffled over with the hood from his grey sweatshirt under his leather jacket pulled over his baseball cap. Shane hadn't worked out in the gym. But he did have to sign some papers for the fight. Cass spent an hour trying to convince him to run, just leave it all behind. And though he tossed around the pros and cons of walking away, they knew he never could.

"What's up?"

"Fuck I'm glad to see you. Why the hell aren't you answering your cell phone? Shit!" Scotty spit on the pavement.

"What is it?"

"I've been looking for you." Scotty said. "I heard what Danny and Mickey did to you. Fuck man, I should have had your back."

"I'm fine."

"There's trouble Shane." Scotty stepped closer.

Shane sighed. "What now? You gambling again? If you are Scotty I swear to God…"

"Nah, I'm cool. But you in some deep shit Shane. Mickey bought a gun."

"Gun?"

"Yes, Andy told me. He bought it an hour ago. Said he'd *be* the Champ soon. Does that mean he coming after you? For what we did? Does it? You need to lay low Shane. You can use my Gram's place. She's in Atlantic City. Go there. Let things cool off and we can tell Higgins."

Shane cut his eyes to the moon. He was sick of hearing lectures from Margene and Cass. He sure as hell wouldn't listen to them from Scotty whose drug and gambling habits forced him to come back. "Fuck Mickey, I'm not running from him."

"Shane!" Scotty grabbed his arm. "He's serious, said he'd kill some black bitch first."

Shane froze. "What did you say?"

"Andy said he talked big about being the Champ, proving you're a loser, dealing with some black broad and getting pay back. He even told Andy you were fucking a cop. Crazy shit man, just crazy!"

"Oh shit. Shit!" Shane put his helmet on. He ignored Scotty and fired up his bike and rode fast out of the alley. Immediately he tried to remember where Raelynn stayed. But his mind went blank. He leaned into his bike and headed for the expressway. "Fuck! Raelynn I'm coming."

CHAPTER ELEVEN

Raelynn entered a cold empty brownstone. She didn't bother to turn on the lights. Dropping her purse and keys she walked through, dazed and disillusioned. Her father had taught her many things. He'd been a great police officer and a fair man. She trusted in the law because of him. But outside of his shadow she'd seen and learned the grey areas of justice. The past forty-eight hours had completely shaken her world. Now she had everything to gain and lose with the decisions she would have to make.

Raelynn started for the bedroom. She paused. An empty Pepsi bottle sat on her coffee table without a coaster. Raelynn never considered herself a neat freak. Not really. But Andrea said she had some real anal-retentive issues. She'd been living in Boston for over three years and nothing in her place looked lived in because she didn't like clutter. Hell she hadn't even hung pictures on all the bare white walls. Deep down she believed Boston would be a temporary stop. Her career would take her to Washington, or maybe New York to work the Homeland Defense unit based there. The few bits of furnishings and personal items she did allow herself to own were always kept in an orderly place. There had been another troubling, unmistakable fact about the bottle of pop left for her. Something she couldn't deny. Raelynn hated Pepsi.

Slow and careful she reached her hand to her hip and released the snap fasten to her holster. How did they break-in? Raelynn remembered her security system had been off for weeks. She had kept meaning to have them come out and check the damn thing. She crept through the house, her gaze lowered to the hardwoods. Slush from the melting snow left wet footprints and a trail toward the bedroom.

Someone had entered her place.

Only a madman would break into a FBI agent's home, have a drink, and leave wet tracks all over their floors. She eased her gun from the holster and headed toward the bedroom. Did the person lie in wait thinking he'd ambush her in the bedroom? Catch her off guard. Of course he did. The scumbag, coward. Well she had a surprise for him.

The door to her bedroom stood partially ajar. Raelynn's steps were silent and precise as she slipped to the left. Any gunfire would call for an immediate drop and counter fire. Most didn't know the best aim and angle of the rooms in their home. However, most people weren't like Raelynn.

It would go down fast when she charged inside. Her heart hammered in her chest. She sucked in a deep breath and blew it out slow. Closing her eyes she summoned control, and then kicked in the door. She swung the gun left then right. The room appeared darker than normal. The blinds were drawn shut. Her eyes did however adjust to the darkness and shadows, though she almost misjudged one and opened fire. Entering she aimed toward the bathroom. With the light on beneath the door she knew the assailant would charge soon.

"Come out or I'll—"

A hand went around her mouth and another pointed a gun to her skull. Raelynn froze. The burglar had been behind her? How was that possible?

"Drop the gun sweetheart. Now."

Raelynn did as she was told.

"Thought you were some hot shit. Huh? Coming in here, heading to the bedroom. Didn't think I knew you'd see the soda? I'm smarter than you bitch. See, people don't think I am, but I am."

Raelynn knew instinctively the informant she hoped didn't recognize her stood in her home. The bastard had followed her? No. He couldn't have. How did he find out where she stayed? Many questions hammered her brain at once. She stood perfectly still with the gun pressed to her temple.

"Yeah, I'm smarter than you. Once I found out your name it was easy babe." She cringed under the wet sounds of his lips smacking. Somehow she'd been set up and the possibilities of why and by whom set her into her a tailspin. "Wondering how I found you huh? Confused? Let me help you out. Couple of internet searches and bam. I got you, you little bitch. Man! Wait until the boss sees you. Now be a good girl. You move or scream I'm dropping you bitch."

Raelynn nodded her obedience.

The hand clasped over her mouth lowered. His revolting touch went to her right breast. She clenched her teeth when she spoke and resisted the urge to slam her fist in his throat. "What do you want?"

"So you fucking Shane? Huh?" he nudged her head with the gun. Raelynn didn't answer. She reserved her answers for the more important questions. The creep squeezed her breast painfully tight as punishment for her silence. She winced. "That fucker cost me respect. I came here to collect some."

"Respect? You turned on your own people and became an informant."

"Shut up!!" he shouted in her ear. "I got plans. And you played right into them. Besides I didn't turn on Ian Higgins. Fucking got busted and set-up. See your sorry-ass boyfriend left me in an alley after the bank job. Those bastards caught me. ATF gave me a deal I couldn't refuse, cause I ain't going to no fucking prison. No fucking way.... Thing is, I ain't no rat either. Now I got me a plan that's gonna work. Damn you're sexy." He began massaging her breast, and pushing his erection into her backside. "Might have me some fun before I waste you."

Raelynn scanned the room for a weapon, for a way out. Unfortunately her nomad style of living left her room nearly bare except for the bed and dresser. The only weapon was her own, a few feet from her.

"I didn't know how to get out of this shit, until I saw you. Then it dawned on me. Shane is the RAT! He's the bastard putting Higgins's operation at risk, not me. I just need to prove it. And I will. Gonna fuck you, kill you, pin this gun here on Shane afterwards at the gym, then give him up to that cold bitch at the ATF. And Ian Higgins will see him as the informant. It's perfect! Perfect!" Mickey laughed. The gun slipped from her temple to her neck. In her mind's eye she knew his trigger finger had either slipped or wasn't positioned. That millisecond of opportunity was all she needed. Raelynn forced his elbow up. Mickey fired into the roof, in surprise. She whirled and slammed her palm upward just beneath his ribcage while twisting his hand in an awkward bend. Something snapped. The gun dropped. Mickey howled in pain and staggered backward. Instead of continuing the fight and giving him time to recover then overpower her, she dropped to the floor and scrambled for one of the guns.

"YOU BITCH I'll KILL YOU!"

There came a single gunshot. Shane bounded up the steps to Raelynn's place. His heart nearly stopped. "Fuck! No. Please God no." He charged the door and found it locked. "Rae! Rae!" he looked back at the street, the silent empty street. The neighbors heard the gunfire. "Shit! Shit!" He kicked the door three times. Under the fourth kick it crashed inward.

With his heart in his throat he rushed inside.

"Come here bitch!" he grabbed at her ankle. Raelynn kicked and crawled, fell, then kicked free of his dragging attempt of her left leg and scrambled away faster. Her hand closed on the gun. Mickey clawed at the air reaching for her. Raelynn rolled to her back and opened fire. Four maybe five rounds blasted in the darkness and the light of gunfire became the strobe to illuminate each shot as it ripped into his chest. Mickey took the fatal blows in the chest, thrown against the shutters covering the window in a macabre dance with his arms flailing and legs buckling. Then both he and the blinds collapsed to the floor.

"Rae!"

Raelynn turned the gun and almost shot Shane in the face. He stood in the door panting. Eyes stretched in shock over what he witnessed. Raelynn captured her breath and Shane flipped up the light switch. Raelynn finally took a breath. Her vision returned to the dead body of her attacker. Blood splatter covered the wall and dresser.

"Sweetheart, Jesus." Shane dropped to the floor reaching for her. She went into his arms but didn't let go of the gun. She needed a moment. Her rational mind hadn't caught up with the savage panic gripping her.

Shane stroked the back of her head. "Are you okay? Please Rae, tell me you're okay."

Raelynn allowed herself three seconds of weakness. It's all the time they could afford. "Go! Get out! Go now!"

"Rae…"

"Shane the cops are on the way. Go, I'll call…um," she struggled to rise. He helped her to her feet. He didn't listen. He pulled her to his chest and held her. God he felt good. She'd never killed a man. Never. She knew the day would come, but she never imagined how empty and scary she'd feel. "Shane you have to go."

"I'm not leaving you." He cupped her face. He kissed her cheeks and at that moment she realized they were wet with tears. Her hands trembled as they clung to him. "I don't care about the cops. I care about you."

Raelynn closed her eyes. She shook her head sadly. "Go Shane."

"Promise you will call me. Promise! He turned and went to the nightstand. He opened it and dug around, finding a pad and pen. He scribbled his number and Scotty's grandmother's address. He'd go there and wait for her.

"Okay, okay." She agreed. "They heard sirens in the distance." Raelynn shoved him toward the door. "Go out the back way. Go now!"

**

Raelynn answered questions from two different detectives. It wasn't until her superiors arrived that the local cops backed off. She sat on her sofa, cold, empty, and mentally exhausted. When she summoned the energy to glance up, she saw the coroner and others taking Mickey's lifeless body out on a stretcher, zipped up in a black bag. She nearly lost it. But the cool glare of Director Melissa Harvey gave her no room for weakness. The ATF and FBI had the place cleared in minutes. Her new partner Kevin Reyes appeared and so did her section chief.

"Care to explain how my informant ended up in your bedroom dead, Agent?" Harvey seethed.

Raelynn recounted the first encounter with Mickey in the alley. She explained the second one at the office earlier today. She didn't know if what he said about how he uncovered her name or address was true, but in the age of technology and thieves it couldn't have been hard for a snake like Mickey. She told them everything except for Shane's appearance. She prayed they didn't put her through additional tests to uncover that truth. He came to help her.

How did he know you were in trouble Raelynn? Ever think to ask? Maybe he was in on it with Mickey? Maybe he was the one who told Mickey who you were.

Raelynn silenced all her doubts and summoned inner control.

Shane had proven himself to be her friend not her enemy. The Director paced in front of her. No one spoke. Then Harvey turned and looked to Kevin Reyes. "We need to contain this. Handle the police. Keep his identity from everyone. Get me the names of every officer that got the call to this shooting. I can't have this getting back to Ian Higgins." Harvey cut Raelynn an angry glare. "Pick up Shane Lafferty and bring him in for questioning."

"Wait!" Raelynn spoke up. Everyone looked to her. She maintained Melissa's stare. "Shane can be useful. Don't spook him by bringing him in."

Harvey smirked. "And how do you suggest we *use* him?"

"Let me talk to him, work on him. Shane has more access to Ian Higgins than your informant. He'll listen to me. If you let me make him an offer he can help us. I know it."

"You know it?"

Agent Kevin Reyes stepped forward. "It's mighty convenient, you killing the informant and now wanting Lafferty to fill his spot."

"You accusing me of something?" Raelynn shouted, a bit of hysteria reached her voice and she immediately regretted it. "You think I set this up?" She rubbed her hands up and down the tops of her thighs. "You think I planned to be attacked and nearly raped?" She seethed, shaking with fury. Harvey and the others studied her. Raelynn pressed her lips together tightly. She turned her gaze to the Director. "I know this is messy ma'am, but you've been on me every step of the way. I didn't set this up. I can help you. I want these men to pay."

"Everyone but Shane Lafferty," Kevin Reyes mumbled.

Melissa Harvey threw up her hand. "That's enough." She

stepped in front of Raelynn. "You have forty-eight hours to save your career young lady. I want something useful before that gun trade goes down. I want Ian Higgins."

"I will need to take Shane to his father. He can give us Ian Higgins. He gave me a message for his son, something to gain his trust. Let me try."

Harvey glanced at Raelynn's section chief who simply nodded. She then turned her gaze to Kevin who looked angry. He'd been kept in the dark. Raelynn never shared this detail with him. He turned and walked out. Harvey cast her a final parting look and the message was crystal clear in her dark eyes. Raelynn had to produce, and she had to produce soon.

Dropping her face in her hands as the others left she allowed herself the minute she needed to breathe. From this moment forward she needed to be clear headed and in control. Shane Lafferty had now become her only hope.

CHAPTER TWELVE

Shane paced. Scotty grew tired of his brooding and left on a beer run. Alone Shane played back the events of the night and its disastrous end. "How did Mickey find her? Dammit!" he slammed his fist into his hand. "No way in hell he should have been able to find her. Could Higgins be on to her? Did Ian send him? Fuck. Fuck!"

A cold sense of dread tightened his muscles. He should have stayed and made sure she was okay. With Mickey dead, more heat than he ever anticipated would come down. He should run. Get his mother and get the hell out of town before Higgins put it all together. The alternative would be prison, or death. If Raelynn confessed to their connection the feds would definitely force her to flip him. He couldn't survive prison with the betrayal of the ITZ branded on his name. He'd be dead in his cell before his bunk got warm.

Shane fled to his cousin's grandmother's house. Scotty should have returned from the store by now. If he hadn't been in shock he wouldn't have let him walk out unarmed. He grabbed his leather jacket but froze at the knock at the door. He removed his gun from his jacket pocket then checked the peephole. Raelynn stood on the other side. She had changed into a chocolate brown leather waist jacket and jeans, with matching leather boots. Her hair looked longer as it lay flat and listless to her shoulders.

He opened the door with anxious hands. She looked up at him then walked in. "You said you would call." Shane tucked the gun discreetly to the back of his pants, before he closed the door.

"You alone?" Raelynn scanned the modest living room, her gaze switched to the dark hall, it led to the bedrooms.

"What? I... um yes, you okay?"

"Good, come with me.'"

"Wait!" he stopped her. Annoyance flared in her dark chocolate eyes. "Are you okay?"

"Am I okay? I nearly got raped, and I killed a man tonight, what do you think?" Her tone hardened.

"Rae... I'm sorry."

"Are you Shane?" she snorted "Really?"

"I didn't mean for you to get hurt."

"Then help me."

"How?" Shane took a step toward her and she in turn stepped back. It hurt to see the distrust in her eyes, but he held his position and didn't advance on her any further.

"Come with me. Now." She said.

Shane walked away. He combed his fingers through his hair. "Turn myself in, you mean? You want me to turn myself in don't you?" He stopped pacing. "I can't. It's not about me Rae, if I do this my mom and my cousin are dead."

"I know." Raelynn's arms dropped from their position, locked and crossing over her breasts, and she lowered her gaze to the floor. She spoke to his shoes instead of him directly. Her voice became soft and remote. "I want you to come with me to see your father. We drive through the night we can get there around four tomorrow."

"It's what? Eighteen hours to drive to Atlanta? Rae I can't spare that kind of time, I've got to train and…" Shane threw his hands up in defeat. Raelynn bit her bottom lip. She refused to look him in the eye. He owed her this. Hell he felt like shit for what happened to her. But a drive to Georgia to see the old man wasn't something he could easily agree to.

"Your father sent a message for you. He said Ian Higgins has a hundred and soon he'll have a hundred more. Do you know what that means?"

"You… saw him?" Shane clenched his fist.

"You know who I am Shane. I made no promises to you."

"Fuck! Why him? Wait. So that's why you're here. So I can get you closer to Higgins. You want the old man to do it? Are you crazy?" he shouted. She didn't give a shit about him. All she offered him was another dead end. And now she wanted to drag him in deeper by involving that bastard sperm donor. He needed to get on his bike and just ride back out of town. Maybe Higgins wouldn't kill his mother. Maybe no one would care. Why the fuck should he?

"Shane. Shane?" She gripped his arm, and he snatched away. Raelynn stepped around him. "Come with me. Your father said he would help us. If you do this we can take evidence to my bosses, something useful and then we can protect your family. The other option is that I take you in. I'll probably be reassigned and you won't be able to see this through your way. "

"Do you know who Rock Lafferty is? No. Neither do I, and that's on purpose. He isn't going to help us. Me and my mom are already marked for death from having the bastard in our lives."

"I met him Shane. I know he's an evil bastard but I saw the look he gave when I mentioned you. He doesn't trust Ian Higgins, something is up with the ITZ."

"What the hell do you know about the ITZ?"

"Let's talk in the car. We got forty-eight hours before they put you in handcuffs. That's all. This is it. This is me believing in you Shane. What are you going to do about it?"

"My mom and cousin? Higgins will find out."

"No. No he won't. The ATF is handling Mickey's shooting. Did you tell anybody about it?"

"No."

"Then we're wasting time. We need to get to Atlanta. Together." She reached and touched his hand. When he didn't respond she clasped his hand and pulled him toward the door. Despite his better judgment he grabbed his jacket and went with her.

Eight hours later and Shane slouched further down in the passenger seat. Raelynn drove at a moderate speed. She didn't speak and neither did he. They were both either too exhausted, or distrustful to try. The only reason he didn't succumb to his fatigue had been her. He kept one eye on her and the other on the road. Several times he allowed his gaze to slip over and linger. Shane admired her strength.

She showed him a small moment of weakness but mostly she held strong. Mickey had certainly rattled her.

"How did you know I was in trouble Shane?" Raelynn asked. The question torpedoed his thoughts.

"Scotty told me Mickey bought a gun. That he was looking for you. I put it together. I wanted to get there in time, I guess I didn't."

"I'm glad you didn't." She glanced over at him. "You're in enough trouble. If you had killed Mickey we both wouldn't have survived the fall out."

"Why? What difference would Mickey's death make to the Feds?"

Raelynn changed lanes. Her hands tightened on the steering wheel and the small sedan accelerated.

"Rae? You want me to trust you then it works both ways sweetheart. Why would Mickey's death matter?"

"He's an informant. He's the one that turned you and Scotty in for the robbery. The ATF got hold of him after the bank heist. Mickey was supposed to help us get Ian Higgins."

Shane laughed. He laughed so hard he began to cough and gasp for air. Raelynn's gaze switched from the road to him in rapid succession. He shook his head at the lunacy. "You guys were going to use Mickey Bryant? The fucker knows about as much of Ian Higgins's business dealings as his gardener."

"He's on his payroll, robbing banks for him." Raelynn stated matter of factly.

"So am I. Soldiers Rae, that's all we are. What Ian's tied to runs all the way to the green hills of Ireland. He doesn't conduct business with his foot soldiers. We aren't privy to his secret deals."

"Then why did he have you rob the bank? For that matter why are you risking so much for him?"

Shane had said too much. He trained his vision on the taillights of the car ahead. The answer to the question she posed could never be easily explained. The reasons why the men in his life made the choices they made were inherent to who they were not what they did. How does a bird explain why he flies, or a lion explain why he roars? Yes he knew right from wrong, but when faced with wrong you just did what comes naturally.

"Dammit Shane, we know you robbed the bank. There's a teller who can identify you."

"Bullshit." Shane scoffed.

"Okay, I'm lying. I don't know what my bosses have on you, but they assure me they have you and Mickey helped them. So why did you rob the bank?"

"Ian wants the money to buy guns." Shane shrugged.

"I know that already."

"I came back to help Scotty. Ian Higgins forced him into some bad shit while I was away. If you met Scotty you'd understand, he's a follower but a good kid. I had to help him. The bank job wasn't my first," He looked over and Raelynn returned her eyes to the road. She wanted him to trust her, then he would. Hell he needed a friend, even if the friend was the same person who could end his life.

"You knew it would end badly for you Shane."

"You knew you could be killed when you joined the F.B.I., did that stop you?" Shane asked.

"Not the same thing." Raelynn's brow furrowed, her gaze switched from the road to him and then back to the road again.

Shane shrugged. "Maybe not. You joined the F.B.I. for your father. I robbed that bank because of mine. There's more things similar between us than not Rae."

"Stop calling me Rae. And we are not alike. I didn't break the law and I never would have. What if a guard surprised you in the robbery or a woman made the wrong move? You would have killed them. That makes us different, very different."

"Care to know what I think?" Shane swung his gaze back to her.

"No."

"Well here it is. I call you Rae because it makes us more than cop and bad guy. That's the place you keep trying to put me so you won't have to admit your real motivation."

"My what?"

"You know damn well I'm more than some case you're working. If not you wouldn't be in this car now trying to save me."

"Save my career," she mumbled. "Not you."

"Keep telling yourself that baby."

"Look Shane…"

"I think that sometimes we do things because we're compelled by something bigger than just right and wrong. It's about loyalty and family pride, or honor or some shit. There is nothing honorable about my family babe, but I'll lay my life down for anybody I care about, including you Rae. If you hadn't killed Mickey, trust me I would have. I'm sorry he hurt you."

Raelynn's knuckles tensed under the strain of her vice grip on the steering wheel. She didn't dare look at him after his confession. The sense of belonging to him felt too strong.

He had been right. She did want to save him. As crazy as it sounded, the idea of him going to prison would be unjust. Inside of Shane Lafferty beat the heart of a man she could love. There would be no future for them. The best she could hope for would be his acceptance into the Witness Protection Program, maybe a fresh start for him. Eventually they would have to say goodbye.

She glanced up at the sign. They'd been on the road for eight almost nine hours and the time on the dash read a little past seven in the morning. The sun hadn't fully risen but the brightness of the day had her eyes watering. If she wanted to make it to the penitentiary before lock down in the afternoon she needed to speed up. Hard to do considering she felt so tired, so soul weary, she could barely keep her eyes open.

"Let me drive." Shane said.

"No."

"Why? We're working on trust here Rae. You need to trust me too. You've been through a lot, more than I'd wish on anyone sweetheart. Let me drive."

Raelynn slipped him a look. She would rather pull over, find a hotel and curl up against his hard chest. But sex would not be an option. In fact she planned to avoid even the mention of sex at all cost. Earlier in the night she picked up on another threat. Her gaze shot up to the mirror. They had a tail. She knew someone had been put on her when she went to pick Shane up. Several times the same unmarked car fell behind then reappeared.

"Rae?"

"Fine," she hit her blinker and exited off the ramp. She drove up to a Chevron and parked near the gas pump. Shane got out before she gave permission or her wishes. Raelynn watched in the rearview mirror as he crossed the back of the car and went to the gas tank. She opened her car door and eased out into the brisk night. The cold felt bitter, dry, and she wished for the warmth of the car immediately. Shane averted his gaze to the nozzle.

She looked away as well. When she started around the car she noticed a sedan pull in and circle to the far right side of the gas station. It parked. The windows had a dark tint making the driver invisible. Still she knew who sat behind the wheel with the car idling. "Kevin." She mumbled under her breath.

"I'll take care of it, get inside." Shane ordered. "It's cold. Do you want something from the convenience store? Coffee?"

"No." Raelynn did as he asked and got back inside of the car. She remained unable to take her eyes off the unmarked vehicle. The Director didn't trust her. Hell she didn't trust herself anymore. If she pulled this off without incident then possibly she could salvage her career. Raelynn reclined the seat Shane had previously warmed. She watched him walk to the mini-mart. His head bowed, his broad shoulders slumped. Her heart again began to ache for him, as did the arousal stirring between her legs. "Dammit Raelynn stop it. You can't possibly still want him. No."

She watched as Shane strolled up and down the aisles. He grabbed a bag of chips and a soda from the freezer, and then bought something in a box from the guy behind the counter. "Yuck. Besides he smokes cigarettes, a disgusting habit."

When Shane returned to the car she pretended not to notice. He flashed her his boyish smile and his eyes glittered with mischief. "You're in my hands now, beautiful."

"Obey the speed limit Shane." She grumbled, a faint smile on her face.

He threw the car into drive and accelerated onto the street. Raelynn closed her eyes. She heard him fiddling with the radio before she fell off to sleep.

CHAPTER THIRTEEN

Raelynn's head bobbed, then rolled as the car jostled her awake. Her eyes opened to the glare of the afternoon sun. She sat up. She'd woken three times during the trip.

The first time was after a brief stop through a drive thru. She ate fries and couldn't stomach the rest. The next time she woke was for a rest stop visit, and then once to make small talk about his choice in music. Mostly she slept. Her body demanded she do so. They travelled through the city on side roads. The navigation system directed their course. She glanced at it and noticed they were only 3 miles from their destination.

"Morning." He said, with a sly smile. "You talk in your sleep."

"I do not." She wiped sleep from her eyes, very conscious of her cottony dry mouth.

"Yes you do. Apparently you've got it bad for me. Kept moaning… Shane, Shane, oh yes baby, Shane… don't stop, lick it, yeah, give it to me. I almost pulled over and…"

"In your dreams." She chuckled. The shared humor between

them faded once the Penitentiary loomed in the distance. "Are you nervous? About seeing him?" she asked.

"No." Shane said dryly.

"You do know I will be present during the meeting. Non-negotiable."

"I figured. I'm telling you the man doesn't want to help you Rae. He wants something else."

"What?" she asked.

"Guess we'll find out." Shane parked. Raelynn snatched down the visor and checked herself in the mirror. She wished she had showered and changed before the visit. She preferred to look more official. But she had been short on time. They had two days before Shane had to turn himself in. This plan of hers had better work. She threw open the car door and grabbed her purse to exit. Shane circled the front of the car in a flash, offering her help. She looked up into his bruised face and again felt warm all over by the tenderness in his eyes. He smiled briefly and held her hand as if she needed assistance. She granted him the permission. Immediately she scanned the parked cars for the one tailing them.

"I ditched him."

"What?"

"The car tailing us, I ditched the bastard and got us here an hour ahead of schedule." Shane grinned.

"Shane I didn't ask you to do that. He was…"

"A Fed. I know. Look I'm doing this with you. Not the people you work for. Not yet. We do it my way. Now come on the bastard will be here soon enough."

Before she could voice her concern he grabbed her hand and pulled her through the gates. They crossed inside and were greeted by the prison staff. She flashed her badge. She didn't have an approved visit so the officials who greeted them had to summon the warden once more. In another hour the prison would lock down and no visits would be granted. They barely made it in time. Shane didn't seem fazed during the wait. He patiently stood at her side as she explained the purpose of their return visit. The warden made a call to her superiors and then granted them thirty minutes. They were soon hustled to the same room she visited with her partner previously, and the wait for Rock Lafferty began. Raelynn stood and paced. Shane sat slumped over with his hands folded on the table. It almost looked like he was praying.

"Are you okay?"

"Do you care?" he answered in a voice distant but tense with restraint.

"Yes. You know I do."

His hard gaze returned to her. The door buzzed, the lock disengaged and Raelynn held her breath as the door opened and the giant of a man with the tattooed skull and angry glare marched in with the aid of the guards. Shane stared up at his father expressionless. Raelynn could swear the air left the room when their eyes met. A flicker of a smile crossed Rock Lafferty's lips and died at the corners of his mouth. The inmate then shuffled over to the chair and sat. He didn't acknowledge Raelynn. He just focused on his son.

"Been a long time Shaney," Rock drawled.

"Wsup? You wanted to meet?"

Rock stared at him.

Shane dropped back in his chair. Raelynn almost spoke to move the conversation along between the men, when Rock Lafferty did instead. He cleared his throat and placed his palms flat to the table. The chains rattled and clanked against the edge. "I said it's been a long time son. You forget about your old man in here? No letters, no visits?"

"Not long enough."

"How's Margene?"

"The same." Shane said.

"I know about your life. She and I speak from time to time."

The admission made Shane go rigid. Raelynn observed the tension now deepening the scowl across his brow.

"How have things been with her? Truthfully?" Rock asked. "I know what you did for your mother. The sacrifice you made. I've tried to reach you but you haven't made it easy. Neither has she. Been here a long time. She could have brought you down to see your old man."

"I'm not here to talk about this." Shane gave a bitter chuckle. "I'm here because the Feds think you want to help them. Give up information on Ian Higgins and the ITZ. Is that true? Are you willing to give them up Dad? You wouldn't fifteen years ago. What's turned you into a rat now?"

Rock sat back, cold rage hardened his features. Raelynn found herself chewing on the inside of her lip until it went numb. The guards at the door looked bored with the entire scene. Rock spoke through clenched teeth. "I'm no fucking rat, boy. I'm your father. Something you seem to have forgotten. I can tell Cass never raised you with a hard hand. Guess that's my fault too. You have no idea what I've given up for you, not them."

"Whatever…"

"You're alive because of me Shaney. No one turns on the ITZ. You know the code. Ian lost sight of his purpose. Shit happens. Give a motherfucker a hundred and he'll take a hundred more. Fuck the Feds. Fuck your mother. I'm talking to you, you're my boy, my flesh and bone and you were supposed to have a chance. Ian robbed you of that and the ITZ silenced me. So I say fuck him too. What I'm about to give you doesn't make me a rat, son. It makes me your father. Thing is Shaney I want something in return."

"Of course you do."

"I want you to get the hell away from Margene and South Boston. I want you to take any deal those Feds give you that will free you, and never look back. Tell me you will Shane."

Raelynn braced for the answer. Silently she prayed Shane would agree. If he did she'd work her ass off to make sure he got the do-over she knew he deserved. She took a step to the side and drew Rock Lafferty's cold glare. She froze. She could now see Shane's face. Tight with conflict and anger she hurt for him, ached to comfort him.

"What's done is done." Shane managed to say under his breath.

"No son. My life's over, I'm okay with that." Rock smiled. An action that made him look even more intimidating. "I've seen you box here under lock up, you should have won that match." Rock grumbled. "You should have been the Champ. Margene and I never gave you a chance to be nothing but what you are, a thief, and a hustler. Time for me to do for you what my old man never did for me. There's a woman named Barbara, she lives in Cambridge near East Eagle Park, call Cass and ask him for the address to Misty Blue. It's what we used to call her. She's from the old neighborhood. You tell her I sent you. You tell her to give you the cannon. She knows what I mean. Don't be stupid about it Shaney. Use this leverage." Another evil grin spread across Rock Lafferty's lips. "Then you send Ian down here to Atlanta, got a bottom bunk for him."

Rock rose. The guards stepped forward. Shane shot up as well. "So that's it? That's all? You got nothing else to say to me."

Rock looked him over. He shrugged. "Your life is your own Shaney. I don't owe you shit."

"Dad." Shane said to his back. "I want to know why? Why did you give it all to Ian and leave Mom and me behind? Why not choose us?"

Rock's shoulders bunched. "I did choose you Shaney." He dropped his head then walked out stiffly.

"You fucking coward!" Shane shouted after him. Raelynn reached for Shane. Her hand rested upon his neck, fingers stretched to reach his jaw. He stood and her hand dropped away. Shane walked out of the room. She hurried her steps and followed him into the hall. Few words of comfort came to mind. Anything she hoped to say would force intimacy between them, which she remained determined to avoid. Instead she went through the motions with him as the prison officials cleared them to leave. She could easily drive back to Boston in shared silence then hand him over to her superiors. Her brain screamed it would be the logical choice. Raelynn cast her gaze over to him. Skin stretched tight across Shane's cheeks and his jaw firmed. His edgy glance slipped her way then returned to the passenger window. Raelynn decided to listen to her heart. "Are you hungry?"

Of course she received no reply. Raelynn drove out to the street and immediately picked up her tail. Agent Reyes had caught up with them. She watched his dark sedan make turn after turn; he did little to disguise his intent. She sensed his impatience by the hurried way he rode her bumper. Soon he'd hit his inside lights and signal for her to pull over. He probably had orders to bring them both in. Raelynn's life and career flashed through her mind. The decision she'd make in the next few minutes would gravely impact both. Her father had been a good police officer. He told her to believe in her instincts when she got accepted into Quantico.

Your instincts will never steer you wrong Baby-Girl.

"Hold on Shane."

"For what?"

Raelynn slammed her foot on the accelerator and shot through the yellow light just as it flashed red. Kevin, in hot pursuit, nearly t-boned a passenger van. She cut down the next street and then the next before taking the entrance ramp to Interstate 20. It was the last she saw of her 'so-called' partner.

Shane didn't flinch. He didn't look back or question her daredevil maneuvers. Raelynn confirmed that Kevin had indeed been left in her dust. She exited the expressway onto Spring Street and drove into downtown Atlanta. She needed a shower, a bed, and food. She hit her turn signal and veered off to a one-way street. Eventually she saw the Westin and drove up into the circular drive.

"Come on Shane. Let's get a bit of rest before we head back to

Boston."

He looked up as if he didn't recognize her voice or where they were. Wordlessly Shane exited the passenger seat and walked into the hotel. Raelynn checked them in under her name.

If she did anything else it would only complicate things further. When questioned by Melissa Harvey she'd say she needed time alone to work Shane to their advantage. Though secretly she hid her ulterior motives even from herself. She would call her office and report in only after she had unchained her heart from Shane Lafferty. If they balked then too damn bad, she felt mentally and physically depleted.

Alone in the elevator with Shane she considered again the words to say to him. He shared so little about himself with her. How could she possibly know or understand his pain.

"You don't have to do this. I know you need to bring me in Rae. Why delay it?" He mumbled when the elevator opened.

"Do what? Eat? Rest? That's all we will do." She walked out of the elevator. He emerged as well, keeping a step behind her. Once she approached the hotel door, she again had to consider the invitation she would be extending by going inside. If she'd been wise she would have reserved separate rooms. But what if he escaped? He wasn't in her custody. He could walk out anytime he chose. No. The logical choice had been the one she made.

"Something wrong?" Shane asked.

"Um, no." she used the key card and opened the door. They walked inside to a cool well made en-suite with a separate bedroom. The draperies were open. She could see the other buildings clustered together to give an imposing night skyline view of downtown Atlanta.

The sun had sunk quickly, another day had gone and she remained unsure of what the next would bring. Raelynn dropped her purse and keys. She turned to ask about ordering food and found Shane directly in front of her.

"Oh, um... maybe we should eat—."

Shane bracketed her face between his hands and drew her lips to his. His sweet breath entered her mouth and she tilted her head back to receive the kiss she had ached for since the moment he rushed in to her townhome and tried to save her life.

Raelynn's lashes lowered in submission, skewing her vision of him. Their connection went from warm and enticing, to fiery hot in an instant. His tongue, quick and fast, darted then swept inside of her mouth. She could barely breathe; she crushed her breasts against his hard chest and clung to him. Raelynn weakened. She savored the sweet taste of him and took in a quivering breath before the kiss ended.

Summoning strength and control over her emotions she gently pushed him off her.

"Don't do that Shane. We aren't going there."

She tried to step around him but his arm slipped around her and hooked her waist. He held her to him. She forgot how good it felt to be held within his powerful boxer's arms. He had the strength of a Viking king and the body to match. She felt all of him under his sweatshirt, and the bulge of his cock to the front of his jeans. Raelynn closed her eyes once more and enjoyed the moment. Shane didn't speak. He let the silence between them settle her doubts before he summoned his voice.

"Why did you bring me here Rae? You have what you want. I'll give you the evidence and turn myself in. It's over."

"Because you're upset, and I'm tired. When we go back to Boston we'll deal with the consequences of our actions. The honest truth is Shane I need a moment and so do you. Sometimes people need to take a breath."

She swallowed hard to mask the nervous quiver in her voice. The truth tasted as sweet as his kiss. It felt good to be straight with him. She however concealed one nugget of honesty. She brought him to the hotel to have him to herself. Melissa Harvey and all those she worked for didn't care about Shane's past or future. They'd squeeze him dry, and once he served their needs, toss him into a system beyond her reach. She could no more guarantee him a deal than she could for herself. Everything felt uncertain. Who could blame her for wanting to stop time, and dance next to that flame of desire he sparked whenever they were together?

"I need you too Rae."

His mouth sought her lips and delivered another hungry kiss. Raelynn's body hummed. The sharp edge of her forbidden desire for this man cut her deep. Weakened under his touch, and roaming hands up and down her backside, she swayed a bit, kissing him harder and longer. To sleep with him again would be disastrous. Wouldn't it?

Shane lifted her to him and instinctively her legs wrapped around his waist, her arms cinched around his neck. She reduced the kiss to soft pecks that soon travelled to his neck. His hard chest swelled and released once her lips grazed his jugular, and he carried her to the bedroom. He lowered her to the bed and she reluctantly released him.

"We can't..." she panted, "We don't have protection."

"I bought some at the gas station," he said, then pressed a kiss to her brow. Dropping a knee to the bed he eased over her.

"What? You did what? Get off me... you planned this?"

He grabbed her wrists and pinned them to the bed. His pelvis and hard cock crushed down on her through his jeans.

"Rae, calm down. I didn't plan to seduce you, but dammit I will always want you. Always. Don't you understand that now? What difference does it make if we have sex because I came prepared or not? We've breeched that boundary, I've had you. And no matter what your mouth says, your pussy wants this even if your heart doesn't!"

Anger glistened in his eyes and his nostrils flared. Admittedly she found his fury sexy, but she knew his last words revealed more than he intended. He believed she just wanted sex. To be screwed by him. He believed her heart felt nothing but pity for him. Truthfully, even now she wasn't quite sure.

Shane stretched his body over her, covering her from head to toe. He pressed his lips to hers again and she was lost. She did want to curl up against him after some hot, sticky, nasty, mind blowing sex. She loved the feel of his cock, the strength of his hips when he slammed inches into her channel. God help her she became so pathetic and weak.

Raelynn tilted her head and her lips opened beneath his. Again his sweet breath from the gum or candy he had hours earlier, slipped in. Her tongue touched the tip of his then retreated shyly. Shane groaned and thrust his tongue deep into her mouth sweeping over the inner crevice while he rocked his hips and cock against the juncture of her thighs. Raelynn wrapped herself around him the way she did when he loved her so hard she thought her spine would cave. With her arms and legs, she held to him tightly, moving beneath him. He kissed her again.

Only the drag of his breath through their kiss filled her lungs. When he came up for air she grabbed his face and forced another kiss on him. Shane kissed her back, but this time kept his lips firmly shut, giving her sweet soft brushes of his mouth over hers. He pulled his head back and stared down at her. The anger on his face and in his voice had melted away.

"Damn woman, you'd make a man walk into a prison and let them slam the doors shut just to have you. Do you understand how hard it is for me now?"

"I've got some idea," she lifted her pelvis to his and rubbed her sex over his bulging cock straining against his jeans.

Shane chuckled. "I think I love you Rae."

Raelynn froze. She knew he'd only shared a joke, but it felt closer to the truth. Her cheeks warmed with shame. She behaved like a hussy each and every time he got between her legs. And she liked it. Love, would never be an option she would choose. Besides, she never fell apart over a man sexually. Usually it was the reverse. But Shane Lafferty had become her new drug.

Slowly she dropped her legs and let go of him.

"Hey," he touched the side of her face. "I was kidding Rae, don't get all serious on me."

"I know." She said.

"I want you, I always do. I need to savor this a bit. Make it last because I believe you."

"Believe me?" Raelynn ask.

"I know this time it's the real deal. The very last time I'll have you. I need something to take with me always."

She opened her mouth to object then shut it. She nodded that she too shared the same feeling. His hand eased between them and plucked her shirt out of its neat tuck into the front of her jeans. As soon as the fabric drew over her stomach his head bowed and his fingers eased down the cup of her bra so his mouth covered her exposed nipple. He used his free hand to rub her between her thighs, stirring heat and desire to the point of suffering.

"You are so damn sexy Rae. I've been wanting to fuck you all morning."

Raelynn rolled her eyes. "I like to think I'd have that effect on you Shane, but you've had more serious things on your mind than me."

He stopped the stroke and flick of his tongue at her nipples. She regretted ruining the moment.

"Look at me." He ordered. Raelynn lifted her gaze to his. "The only way I held it together today was because of you." Shane's gaze lowered to her nipple glistening now from his sweet licks. He touched her pussy once more, cupped it in the palm of his hand. He stroked her center making her moist and hot for him. "Damn I want to rip these jeans off you right now," he mumbled.

"Go for it," she chuckled.

A wicked grin spread over his mouth. Raelynn reached and released the top button of her jeans. She slowly eased down her zipper. She could push her jeans off her hips and grant him full access but she knew he craved the tease. He knocked her hand away and ran two fingers along the top trim of her panty, then eased his calloused fingers underneath. They grazed her mound with necessary roughness, and then slipped to her swollen folds. The abrasive feel of the pads of his fingers along her inner most walls melted her inside and she creamed herself. Raelynn's lashes fluttered then shut.

The same two fingers boldly plied open her pussy while another pierced her cunt. She gasped silently, her hips lifting from the bed. Instinctively she thrust her pelvis upward wanting him to drive his finger deeper.

"You like that don't you, when I fuck you with my finger? Should I use my tongue instead? Pussy so damn sweet I could eat it all day," he groaned.

Raelynn's head dropped to the left then the right, her hips rotated and his fingers screwed deeper into her channel. "I don't want your tongue," she bit out. "I want you!" She said through clenched teeth. He didn't respond. The urge to be filled with him became so overwhelming she shuddered through another release. She heard him chuckle at her weakness and her pride burned her chest and cheeks. Her eyes flashed open. She shoved him off.

Surprise removed the humor from his eyes. Shane shifted away and withdrew his hand. Raelynn slipped to the floor. She got on her knees before him. Seated, feet firm to the floor; Shane leaned back and rested his weight on his hands at his sides. She swung her gaze upward and caught the curious glint of anticipation in his stare. Raelynn felt the inside of her mouth water. She removed his long coiled cock from the front of his zipper. His fingers dug into her hair and grazed her scalp, as if trying to rush the inevitable. She had every intention of sucking his cock until he begged for release. Her rapid breathing seemed to match his. Her fingers closed around the base of his shaft and her mouth covered the arrowed point of his cock-head then sank lower. Thick hardness pushed down her tongue and stretched her jaws. She sucked and drew him in deeper.

Aroused by his male scent and soft grunts of pleasure she withdrew several inches to stroke her tongue along his length. Raelynn wanted to burn every inch of him into her memory. His scent, his taste, and the tight hard steel in her mouth made it possible. Suctioning hard she worked her fist up and down his shaft driving pleasure and deep moans from him.

She peeked up. His head fell back. Shane's Adams-apple bobbed in his throat, his jaw clenched. It got so good to him he began to crank his hips, drilling his cock steadily to drive himself deeper. He thrust past her tongue and hit the back of her of throat making her convulse with him. But she held on tighter and kept sucking the thick veined length of him in and out of her mouth until her jaws tensed and her eyes watered under the strain.

A cry of his submission gusted above her. She gripped his balls and squeezed with her free hand knowing his eruption could come unexpectedly premature, and soon. As if understanding his limit he pushed her back gently then fell on the bed with his cock pointed north. His hand covered hers ringed tightly around his shaft to stop her from stroking.

"Damn Rae, stop. You're killing me. I don't want to come yet."

Raelynn loosened her hold then pulled her hand away. She wiped at her mouth with the back of her hand. Slowly she straightened and stood before him. Shane groaned massaging his angry erect cock. Raelynn undid the buttons to her shirt. His lids slowly parted and he stared up at her. He appeared too weak with need to rise. So she took her time and removed her shirt then bra.

Raelynn pushed her jeans down the heart shaped curve of her hips and made sure to sway them lightly as she did so. A sly smile eased over Shane's lips and she felt heat and moisture build between her inner folds.

"Condom?" she asked.

His gaze switched to his crumbled jacket on the side of the bed. In nothing but her panties she walked over and removed the box from the inside pocket. She smiled at the black and gold labeling. "Magnums, you are a big boy aren't you?" She chuckled.

Shane grinned. "The biggest and the baddest baby."

Raelynn stepped between his legs and reached down to sheath his cock. Shane put his hands behind his head and observed. The hunger and lust banked in the heated stare he gave her made her cunt throb. She almost reached and touched herself. She resisted.

Careful of her handling of him, she dropped a knee on the left side of his hip and then the other to straddle him. She reached between her legs and parted the lips of her vagina, guiding the head of his cock to her opening. Shane grabbed her hips to steady her glide downward.

Raelynn was grateful for the assistance. Her lower half shook so hard she thought she'd drop and miss her target over her excitement. Instead she sank down on raw power. Shane drove his hips upward and filled her completely. Raelynn hissed between clenched teeth and then rolled her ass to take him deeper.

Raelynn fell forward and her nipples grazed his chest, sending shivers of pleasure down her spine. Her hands braced against his hard biceps. She bounced on his cock, never breaking eye contact with him. Shane gripped both halves of her ass and parted her plump buttocks to keep her open and accessible as she rose up and down on his length. Tiny quivers of pleasure sparked along her inner channel. His bottom maneuvers had him tunneling upward deeply.

"Yeah, Rae, like that, fuck... fuck... girl it's good."

She loved his torment. It helped soothe hers as she fought back the orgasmic spasms to stay in control. She dug her nails into his chest, now sweating and heaving with his deep intakes of breath. She pumped her hips then rolled her ass and bounced harder and harder. Shane groaned deep in his throat. Every muscle in his jaw and neck tensed and tightened. She leaned in, never breaking rhythm to kiss his fading bruises along the side of his face. God she could do this all night.

Raelynn pushed her lips to his ear and spoke through her own deep pants. "Fuck me Shane, fuck me now."

Shane obliged. He flipped her to her back and rammed himself deep. She cried out in surprise. Her nails drew red welts down his back. He hooked one of her legs over his arm and began to thrust his cock with consecutive slams into her tight hole and she felt her body accommodate the invasion.

He glared down at her with a mixture of desire and rage. His repeated thrusts caused the headboard to knock against the wall. Raelynn grabbed his hair and yanked hard to bring his face from her neck and then slammed her mouth to his. She bit Shane's lower lip, and sucked it in her mouth, loving the sound of the helpless moans escaping him. The kiss they shared was a duel of tongues and clashing of wills. She clung to him as he power drilled his cock in and out of her with relentless fury. She felt her entire being ignite with excitement and pleasure. It came in hard crashing waves over her.

"I want to fuck you, let me," he panted.

At first she didn't understand his wish. Was he not already fucking her senseless. Then he withdrew prematurely. She was only seconds from a climax. She cried out in frustration.

Shane guided her over to her stomach; her legs fell over the side of the bed. He slipped his hand underneath her abdomen and drew her up so that her knees were firm to the bed and her legs splayed apart. Raelynn gripped the sheets, keeping her head bowed. Without warning or preparation he slammed back into her cunt and she bit through the sheet to the mattress.

"This is me fucking you Rae," he grunted. He slammed into her again and then pinched her clit until her entire pussy went into distress. He stood behind her with his hand holding her left shoulder and his other at her hips. He rocked his cock in and out of her with long coaxing strokes, and then pumped his hips to drive several long inches deep. She answered his passion with her own, rolling her ass against his pelvis and lower belly, allowing him to screw her deeply. The pump action of his hips became erratic and she felt his own control slipping. Raelynn closed her eyes to it all and then let him take her to the brink.

Several hard, quick, jerky thrusts and they both crashed on the bed. Shane kept thrusting, fucking her against the side of the bed until they exploded in perfect harmony.

CHAPTER FOURTEEN

Shane found it impossible to move. He collapsed on top of her back, shuddering hard. His groin melted in her heated, steamy channel. She didn't speak and suddenly he feared his aggression had been too much. He summoned the strength to disengage from her. Raelynn crawled from him to the center of the bed. Shane joined her. He panted and waited for his heart to stop racing. Raelynn rolled over to him, her arm eased around his waist. She kissed his chest. "That was amazing."

"Did I—"

"Hurt me? Yes. Hurt me soooo good!" she laughed.

He shook his head smiling. "You are one hell of a woman Rae."

Her head shot up. "I used to hate when people called me Rae, or abbreviated my name. It really pissed me off when you picked up the habit. Now, I swear Shane you make me go against my nature. Isn't that strange?"

He touched the side of her face. "No. Nothing about us is strange to me. We fit, don't we Rae? You see it, I feel it too."

"Sexually, yeah, we're compatible." She snuggled him and his smile faded. *What did she mean sexually?* Why did she feel the need to always downgrade every emotion to the sexual bullshit? He felt his chest tighten with anger. It had been a shitty day, a bullshit life. Raelynn had been his only bright spot and she'd couldn't or wouldn't grant him the truth. It had to be more than sex between them. He'd had enough pussy in his lifetime to know the difference. He let her go and turned away.

"Hey wait, I'm not done with you mister."

"Let go babe."

Raelynn frowned; with no other choice she released him. Shane ripped the sheet from his waist and stormed off to the bathroom. The door slammed harder than he intended. He didn't care. He peeled off the condom and tossed it to the toilet. When he turned to flush it down he glimpsed his reflection from the corner of his eye. The bruises, the scars, they were a telltale sign of his inner pain and conflict. He looked like shit and he felt even worse.

"Shane?" Raelynn rapped on the door. "Can I come in?"

Shane leaned forward on the sink. He stared at his reflection. He found little redeemable in the man staring back. He drew in a deep, sharp breath, not liking the vulnerability clinging to his masculinity like a second skin. All for a woman way out of his league.

"Shane?"

The door slowly opened. Ruthlessly he turned his gaze toward her once she entered the bathroom. She closed the door behind her meeting his stare. Shane swung his gaze back to the mirror. He resisted the urge to slam his fist dead in the center of the glass. Shatter the illusion of control and break her hold on him. He'd seen his father. The bastard he'd loved and missed all his childhood, turned cold-blooded murderer. Shane shuddered with disgust over the emotion Rock Lafferty brought to the surface. "I think I'm in trouble Rae, you need to give me a minute." He mumbled.

"No." She said defiantly.

He closed his eyes. He couldn't look at her. He needed a moment. His pride forbade him from asking again. She'd know how weakened and unsure he'd become. Instead he dropped his head and mourned his existence.

"Shane? Talk to me?" she touched his back.

When he didn't respond her small hand went up and down his spine with such tenderness he felt some of the sadness strangling his heart abate. "Shane, listen to me. There is a way out of this mess. I will help you find it."

"What if I don't want your help?" he said through clenched teeth. His eyes flashed open and his gaze latched on to hers through the reflection in the vanity mirror. "What if I just want you?"

Her hand dropped away. "I don't understand?"

"The fuck if you don't! You feel it too Rae. I can't just fuck you and not feel anything. Trust me sweetheart I've tried. You make me want more."

"I... I—"

"Dammit Rae, don't play me! This game between us has to stop."

She crossed her arms over those beautiful breasts of hers and it aroused him. Damn. She could pick her nose and he'd be turned on.

She made him fucking crazy and he was beginning to believe she did it on purpose.

"You're right. Because *this* was a mistake." She said flatly.

"So was my conception. Can't undo it though, now can I? And you can't undo fucking me, liking it, risking your career for dick!"

"Careful Shane, I won't stand for you talking to me that way!" she shouted at him. Her nostrils flared and her eyes narrowed into angry slits.

He made her mad. Good! Now she knew how fucking frustrated and hopeless he felt. Shane dropped his head and shook it. *Jesus Christ.* How did he end up here? Scotty called and begged for his help. The next thing he knew he wore a mask of a dead president and held a gun in the face of a bank teller. In the end he'd fucking lost his balls over a federal agent with a hard-on for his dick and nothing else. Even now he secretly prayed she'd give him a chance. "I'm not alone in this Rae. I don't give a shit what you say, this isn't just about sex."

"Well hell Shane, what do you expect from me? You're a criminal for pete's sake."

"And you're a heartless bitch!" he shot back.

Raelynn's eyes stretched. He regretted his outburst the moment it slipped out of his thoughtless lips. He had no experience with being vulnerable. He couldn't break himself down any further and not lose control. He turned to face her fury. "Rae, I'm sorry…."

"Go to hell you scumbag!" She turned to escape him and he threw his hand to the door to trap her in. She shot him a murderous glare.

"Rae, please. I'm sorry okay? I just. I'm losing it here. I didn't mean it. I apologize."

She didn't budge. He her eyes, glistened with hurt and angry tears. *So she did have feelings?* "No matter what card I play with you I lose. You give me a taste of heaven then dismiss it when I say I want more. I need something...."

"Exactly. You need something. Not me. I could be anyone and..."

"No dammit! It's you. It's us. I need us."

Raelynn stared at him. "How am I supposed to play this out Shane? What options in this do I really have? We barely know each other."

"But our lives have been thrown together in days. You saved my life in the alley behind Gladiators." He stroked her cheek.

Her beautiful eyes lowered under her dark lashes. "You tried to save me when Mickey broke into my place."

"We fit Rae. Maybe it's too soon to say we can fall in love, but we've been through some tough shit together. There's something between us. All I want is for you to admit you feel it, something more than pity."

She stood beneath him a foot shorter. Her back pressed to the wall, her sexy body flush and on display. He hedged his touch and then pressed his palm to the side of her face. "I'll do it. I'll give the Feds what they want, but I want something in return. I want you Rae."

"Me?"

"I want you." He said, pressing a kiss to her lips. He pushed up against her and her soft breasts cushioned his weight. "Yes, Rae, I want you. All of you," he slipped her some tongue.

"You expect me to fuck you after you called me a bitch?" she shoved him back.

"No. I expect you to let me make love to you." He heaved her up against the door. She wrapped her legs around his waist. His cock rose to duty. Shane thrust the head into her tightness and she stopped him. "No. We need a condom."

"Forget the condom." He gave her another deep thrust.

"No Shane! I don't want a kid. I'm not on the pill. Stop!"

He let her go. He stepped back a little embarrassed over his behavior. He could tell her that she'd already had his bare dick, but she'd probably go nuts. She stared at him and the hard judgment on her face softened. "I'll admit that I'm attracted to you. The sex is great, and I... I've started to care for you. But I can't and I won't lead you to believe in a future we won't have Shane. I'm not a cold-hearted bitch. If I lied to you that's what I'd be. This ends, when the sun comes up. Those are the rules."

She walked out of the bathroom.

Shane groaned. He stepped back and leaned against the sink. "Didn't they tell you babe, I don't follow the fucking rules." He mumbled under his breath.

Room Service was quite tasty. They ate cheeseburgers and garden salads in bed, while watching TV. The hour grew late before she realized it. They didn't make love. Though she wished he'd make a move on her, he never did. He talked a bit about his childhood. She told him about hers. Though their father's were polar opposites the bonds they shared with their dads, as children were the same. It puzzled her.

The night ended with him resting against her breast while she talked about the first time she handled a gun on a hunting trip with her dad, to the last time she fired one at her attacker. She too drifted to sleep, then woke shortly after. Raelynn looked over at him while he slept and then back to the news broadcast on the television. She tossed the covers and eased out from under.

Raelynn found her panties and pulled them up. She cast her gaze back to the bed. He looked absolutely beautiful. His body rippled with muscles but not overly done, he had the disheveled look of a gladiator or warrior from another time period. She lied to him earlier. Her reasoning had been sound. Hurt him now, instead of later. Of course she wanted more, and it wasn't about sex. The man made her feel alive. With him things were basic. Man, woman, they were just two people who connected. But to think of or wish for anything else with him would be foolish.

Raelynn walked out of the bedroom into the suite. She found her jacket and retrieved her cell phone. The flashing light on the surface made her heart drop. She rubbed her finger over the LCD and brought up the screen. She'd missed sixteen calls. Raelynn sighed. She could call in and face the ire of her superiors or delay it until they left. Either choice would seal her fate. She tossed the phone and dropped her face in her hands. She'd dug a hole, a deep one. There would be no going back after this.

She picked up the phone and called the one person who could understand.

"Hello?"

"Hi Dad."

"Raelynn, how are you baby girl? I was just telling your mama that I needed to call you."

"I'm good Daddy. How are you? How's Mom?" She slumped back on the sofa.

"She misses you. I've told you to call home more."

Raelynn smiled. "Sorry. Been busy."

"Big things happening in Homeland Defense?" She could hear the excitement and pride in his voice. He bragged on her constantly. She would call him and even discuss closed cases with him. Most of them weren't hers, but Raelynn observed and learned from everything around her.

"I got a case, it's a joint one with the ATF."

"Wow! Way to go baby girl. I'm so proud of you."

Raelynn's gaze cut back toward the door where her sleeping bad boy lie. "I was hoping to get some advice Daddy."

"Go for it. Lay it on me."

"A bad guy, bank robbers, extortionist, this case is connected to one of he evilest men in the city of Boston. May even have a political fallout."

"Sounds serious. Why the ATF?"

"Guns."

"Right. Right."

Raelynn slumped forward. "Thing is, there's a suspect in the robbery who isn't really a bad guy. What I mean is I think he can break the case if we give him a chance. My superiors don't care or think so. My instinct says I should help him."

"An informant?" her father asked.

"Yes." Raelynn said softly. She closed her eyes and shoved down her emotions. "But he's not clean Daddy. He's done bad things too. I'm taking risks in trying to push for him to receive a deal. I'm so new at this I don't want to make the wrong choice." She bit her lip to keep from saying she feared she already had.

Her dad remained silent a moment and then he spoke. "The world isn't black and white Rae, but the law is. You sometimes have to work in shades of grey to get justice. If helping this informant within the law brings justice to the victims of this evil man you speak of, then yes you must do it. I have a question."

Raelynn braced for it. She was grateful for the call instead of a face to face with her father. He knew her well, and would probably suspect her attachment to Shane. Even now she hated herself for letting things advance so far. "Go ahead Daddy."

"Why this informant Raelynn? What makes him different?"

"I don't know Daddy. I really don't."

"Then it is your instinct, and I trust it Raelynn, you need to learn to."

She smiled. "I love you."

"Call your mother. Soon."

"I will I promise."

"Bye baby girl."

"Bye."

Raelynn sucked in a deep breath and released it. She rose and returned to her lover.

CHAPTER FIFTEEN

Shane smiled when petal soft lips brushed along the column of his neck to his chin. A warm lush body covered his. In his dreams it had been Raelynn. He opened his eyes and found his desire had become his reality. She stroked his penis until his erection filled her hand, and then rolled a condom on.

Before he could say a word his mouth fused with hers. He ran his hands down the curves he'd kill a man for, then up her backside under the cover of the sheets. Shane rolled her to her back.

His tongue probed and swept her mouth. He owned their kiss. He lifted his mouth from hers to look upon her face. His ass rose under the sheet and he dragged his rock hard cock up for the strike. Raelynn's small pink tongue slipped out and licked her bottom lip. Her irises blazed amber brown with excitement, she joined her hands behind his neck. Her knees dropped further apart and her ass lifted from the mattress forcing his cockhead to sink an inch into her opening. Her core seemed to vibrate around the ring of his cock and he nearly lost control. The burning ache for her wouldn't relent. Shane plunged deep.

The latex sheathing his cock did little to mute the hot, wet, tightness of her channel. Damn he wished he could take her without one. The pleasure would be cataclysmic.

"Now baby! Now!" Raelynn grunted in frustration. Shane realized he hadn't moved, he lay on top of her, buried to the hilt. Shane dragged his cock out several inches then lunged his hips forward and pummeled her pussy with repeated strikes. He used his knees to roughly spread her thighs even further apart.

"My pussy, mine, mine, mine," he groaned moving beyond his control. He braced a hand to the headboard to balance his weight and rolled his hips, then gave her repeated strikes of his dick. The steamy heat of her clenching channel sent spasms through his erection. He flexed his hips and thrust harder and harder. "Fuck! Holy fuck!!" he cried out throwing his head back and squeezing his eyes tightly shut.

Raelynn's nails scraped down either side of his back and the sting extended to his buttocks, she gripped it tightly. Shane drew in a short pained breath, she had become too much. She moved that sexy ass of hers and her tight nipples circled his chest. "Fuck!" he growled, screwing her with every rigid muscle below his abdomen.

It felt as if her entire body quivered and she sighed instead moaned. The vaginal walls clenched around him melted and he dropped on her pounding away at his climax until the reservoir of his condom overflowed. "Yes! Yes! Yes!" he heard himself grunt through prisms of pleasure swirling around his cock and his pelvis, then arrowed up through his stomach to pierce his heart. It didn't matter how crazy it sounded he was in love.

Raelynn giggled under his crushing weight and he lifted to be sure to give her room. "You've done me in," he half-joked. Suddenly he wanted to know her sexual past. He wanted the names and numbers of any man who had ever breached her honey walls so he could drag their asses into the ring and extinguish them.

She rolled to his chest. "We have to go Shane. It's time. I had forty-eight hours to bring you back. Let's see, it's just two in the morning. We leave now we can make it to Boston around seven tonight."

He closed his eyes struggling to catch his breath.

"Shane?"

"I hear you Rae. Give me a minute."

"We can shower together. You get your noodle up and you can fuck me. In the ass if you like?"

His eyes flashed open.

She laughed. "Just kidding!" she tried to flee the bed. Shane grabbed her, his cock now semi-erect. "No Shane!!" she screamed, "I was just kidding!"

"I'm not," he kicked open the door to the bathroom. He'd wanted to sink his cock in her round ass since the first time he saw it in a pair of blue jeans. Nothing would prevent him from the opportunity. Raelynn giggled. Damn this woman. She was killing him.

**

The drive back had been quicker than either of them expected. They listened to music and argued over Blues and Blue Grass. Shane forced her to listen to a few Blue Grass stations and to her surprise she liked it. He talked a lot more. Told her of his first crime. How he and his crew did a bunch of smash and grabs at local stores in the mall. He hustled the stolen goods in Southie and made money to keep the lights on for his mother. Eventually the conversation veered to the bitterness he harbored for his father. Shane confirmed what Raelynn suspected. Rock Lafferty once had more power and influence than he let on. He gave it all up for the ITZ, leaving Ian Higgins in charge. The reasons why his father would leave them penniless baffled Shane, but he suspected his mother being Ian's whore behind his father's back had been part of the cause. Shane grew silent after the revelation.

"Cass gave me the address. I know where we can find her."

"Who?" Raelynn asked.

"Cass, my trainer. Remember the guy that threw you out of the showers? He knows this woman. If the old-man is right we should go to her first. Then you take me in."

"But, I can't. My boss's orders were clear. They want you brought in immediately."

Shane cut her a look. Raelynn bit down on her bottom lip. "You aren't trying to back out of this are you?"

"No Rae. My word is my bond. Take me to her and let me finish this. Then we'll do it your way."

Raelynn sighed. "Shane you can just about convince me of anything."

"Not anything." He mumbled casting his gaze away. She ignored the comment. He keyed the address into the navigation system and they coasted in silence on the highway and back streets until they arrived at her doorstep. When she turned off the car she sucked in a deep breath and said what she'd been holding back for an hour. "Shane? I do care, more than I should."

"I knew it." He mumbled, throwing open the door.

Raelynn glared and he shot her a wink over his shoulder before he got out and slammed the car door. Raelynn retrieved her gun from the glove compartment and hurried to follow him. She slipped the gun in the back of her pants under her leather jacket.

A very attractive woman met them at the door. With creamy white skin and pale blonde hair she looked maybe five years younger than Raelynn assumed was her actual age. "Come inside! Quick!" she said, her eyes darted to the street. Raelynn kept her hand to her back and on the gun. She felt a setup but didn't know why. Shane bristled with tension as well. They both entered the home on guard. The woman hurried away from the vestibule, moving deeper into her barely lit house. Raelynn considered all the protocol she'd broken. She should have called this in. What was she thinking?

"Why? Why the hell did he give your mother my number? Do you know she's called here twice to threaten me! Damn him. He could have called me instead of her."

"My dad called my mom?" Shane asked, baffled.

"He wanted her to help you find me, in case Cass came down with amnesia. She said you were bringing the Feds!" The woman shot Raelynn a withering glare. "Look, my life is different now. I don't deal with men like Rock Lafferty. I have a career, respect, and friends. I don't want any part of this shit, and nothing to do with the ITZ."

"We aren't here to hassle you." Raelynn volunteered. "We can keep your name out of the investigation."

The woman glared at her. "Kiss my ass Fed. I know what you're here for!"

Shane stepped in front of Raelynn. He towered over the frightened lady. "Give us the cannon. Dad said you knew what that meant. Give it to us and we'll go."

"Damn right you will. And take that bitch with you." She turned and went to the six-foot tall china cabinet pushed against the wall. She opened the bottom drawer. Raelynn stepped from behind Shane to be sure the crazy lady didn't draw a weapon. Instead she revealed a camera, a professional one. "Here! Take the damn thing! Tell your father I've done all I will do, and to never bother me again."

"A camera?" Shane frowned. Staring at it.

Raelynn rolled her eyes and accepted it. "It's probably what's on the film that we need Shane. She flipped it over and released the latch to unwind the film. She dropped the roll out and into her palm.

Shane looked back to the woman for an explanation. "How do you know my father? Why would you keep this for him?"

The woman refused to answer. It pissed Raelynn off. "I suggest you answer him, or we'll have to dig a bit more to find out exactly why you and Rock Lafferty are connected."

The woman sighed. She spoke through clenched teeth. "I used to dance at Foley's, back in the eighties, before it turned legit. Your dad and I were friends. Your mom was and is a crazy bitch. She found out about your dad's frequent trips to Foley's and waited for me one night. She hit me in the face with a wrench. I lost all my front teeth. That's how I know your crazy parents."

"Then why did you keep this?" Raelynn pressed. "Why do anything for Rock Lafferty?"

"Rock did favors for people. He paid my medical bills and got my teeth fixed. He even set me up with a little money so I could go to school. Yes strippers do go to college." The woman huffed, and crossed her arms. "Rock could make things happen."

"Moreso than Ian Higgins?" Raelynn pressed.

The woman averted her gaze. "I won't talk about Ian or the ITZ. I'll tell you this. I got in a tight spot some years ago even after I left the life. I needed help. Rock made things right for me, but I was out of my free passes with him. He told me for payment I had to hold on to that fucking camera until he sent for it. Two weeks later he got busted for killing those Lithuanians. That camera has been here ever since."

"And you just kept it? Never developed the film?" Raelynn asked.

The woman gave her an incredulous look. She cut her angry gaze over to Shane. "Talk to your Fed here and tell her how things work. I wouldn't touch the thing! To know what's on that film is a death sentence I'm sure."

Shane nodded. He switched his gaze to Raelynn. "She's right. I think we should leave." Shane turned and walked out. Raelynn followed. Once they were in the car she spoke.

"Why did your father call your mother? I thought they were estranged?"

"We'll have to ask her that. Every day I know less and less about my parents."

She bit down on her tongue to stop the questions, but still she had to ask more. "Shane what if your father didn't kill those Lithuanians? What if he was set up?"

"My father is no angel. You heard her."

"He's not stupid either Shane. He gave her a camera probably loaded with information that could sink Ian Higgins, maybe even the ITZ. We should…"

"It's done Rae! Dammit, I'm sick of this find the clues shit. Take me in."

Raelynn shook her head. "This is your life Shane. You heard your father. Take control of it. Stop sulking over how your parents failed you and fight for your life dammit!"

Shane wiped his hand down his face. "What is there to find Rae, more bullshit? I've lived it. I'm tired of it."

"No you're afraid of something. Tell me what it is?" Raelynn insisted. "Tell me Shane."

He spoke through clenched teeth. "Barbara wasn't paranoid. She was scared. The ITZ isn't some street gang. They're powerful. They won't care that you're a federal agent. Do you understand? Give the photos to your bosses and walk away. Get off this case. I can't… if things go bad, I can't protect you."

Raelynn frowned. She looked over and realized for the first time he wasn't upset over his parents, or even his safety. He'd been fighting her to keep her clear of this organization. "Shane I…"

"I'm serious Rae. You said it yourself we have no future. Hell we don't know where I will end up. I don't want you hurt."

"Then free yourself. Let's find out why the Lithuanians were murdered. Let's…"

"No. No dammit. You don't listen Rae. Give them the film and I'll turn myself in. I won't name my cousin. Only me. I'll go down for the robbery and take Mickey's good name with me."

"I haven't worked the deal out completely. They'll arrest you and lock you up, maybe for life. I can't protect you like I promised. And just like you, I can't sit back and see you hurt. I won't do it."

"Fine. It's not your job to save me. I'm not safe on the streets. Take me in and let the Feds do what they do."

"No." She slammed her foot down on the brake pedal. Raelynn swirled the steering column and sped down the next street. "I have a plan."

"What the hell are you doing?"

"Going to see a friend. She can help us." She shot Shane a glare. "And you will help me. Do you understand?"

Shane said nothing. Raelynn's heart raced. Her dad said she should trust her instincts. She prayed her instincts were right about Shane Lafferty.

CHAPTER SIXTEEN

Raelynn called a woman named Andrea. It wasn't until they arrived on her friend's doorstep did Shane recognize the babe. The night he first met Raelynn her friends had surrounded her. He did notice this particular wild beauty with the auburn dreadlocks as she danced the night away. Andrea had skin a shade darker than Raelynn's, and a pair of the roundest deep-set brown eyes under long lashes.

Curvy, she wore a cream sweater that had a furry look with a deep V-neck that barely contained her heavy bust, and a long multicolored skirt that brushed the floor when she stepped back.

Inside her home Shane felt bowled over by its warm eclectic charm, which fit the artsy type of personality she exuded. Walls were painted in striking bright colors of deep magenta, green, yellow and purple. Sculptures and paintings consisted mostly of black men in nude shots, all of which shared a familiarity that hinted the same artist had done each.

She turned and granted them both entrance. Her gypsy skirt swirled around her bare feet. If Raelynn hadn't made him her bitch, he'd definitely have gone for this one. Though he loved curves on women, his desire for black women had been a recent occurrence.

"So who is the cutie Raelynn?" Andrea cast her gaze back over her shoulder and narrowed her penetrating stare.

He felt his cheeks warm with a deep blush. This beauty had just as much confidence as Raelynn, but definitely preferred to dominate her men. He felt like a fly being invited to tea by a black widow spider. The door closed behind him and he had to smile back at Raelynn. Who were these women? He'd had his prejudices of others. Hell he grew up in a very segregated, closed community. He never met women more confident and aware than these two. It fascinated and unnerved him.

"'His name is Shane, Andrea, please behave."

Andrea laughed.

"I need a favor." Raelynn said.

"Okay?" Andrea sat on her sofa. Shane lowered into the chair across from Andrea and Raelynn stood.

"Need you to develop some 35 mm film for us. Now."

"Really?" Andrea asked, never taking her eyes off Shane. "How retro."

"I'm serious."

Andrea slipped Shane a sly look. "Some naughty pictures I hope?" Andrea drew in her bottom lip as if tempted by the mere idea. "I'm curious Shane, what happened to your face?"

Shane tensed. He forgot about the bruises. His face no longer ached in remembrance as it had the past few days, and he'd taken off the bandage that covered the crudest scar next to his left eye. He nearly touched the tender spot under the ladies' watchful stare. "Fell off my bike." He lied.

Andrea's brow winged up. "Motorcycle?" She dropped a hand

on her hip. "That's hot. Completes the bad boy vibe you got going on."

"Andrea!" Raelynn's disapproval sharpened her tone. "No time for games."

Andrea laughed again. Her laughter actually eased the tense knot of dread Shane had been carrying like a stone around his neck. His mouth twitched and he realized he was smiling.

"Just having fun with him. He looks like he's about to jump out of his skin. Is he an undercover or something?"

"Stop flirting. I'm serious." Raelynn mumbled.

Andrea swung her gaze left to Raelynn, then back to Shane, then back to Raelynn. "Wait, you two… nah, not your type. Raelynn likes the button down, stiff, up the butt guy. Now me? I'm very flexible."

Shane laughed and it was indeed awkward. Andrea and Raelynn stared at him. Their host slapped her hands to the top of her thighs and rose. She and Raelynn walked off toward the kitchen. He could hear their hushed argument. Andrea then let go a deep laugh. Shane could guess the reason for the humor.

Whatever Raelynn confessed had her friend laughing for a straight minute. She walked back out and Raelynn's face went tight with shame. "Well Shane, make yourself comfortable sweetie. I won't be long." She shot Raelynn a mocking wink then laughed some more before she headed to the stairs of her basement.

Raelynn snatched off her jacket, clearly upset. "Don't say a word."

Shane leaned forward. "We going steady Rae?"

"In your dreams playboy." She picked up her phone and called someone. Shane tuned in on her clipped conversation. Raelynn spoke in three word sentences, revealing little. She then gave the address to Andrea's place before she ended the call.

"Who did you call?" Shane asked.

"Reinforcements. Whatever we find on those pictures we'll use as leverage, but I need to do some damage control for ditching my partner. If my plan is going to work we get one shot at this, so we have to do it right."

Shane rose. "I need to make a call myself."

"Wait...where are you going?"

"Just outside. You trust me right?"

Raelynn blinked up at him. He shook his head to reassure her. "I'm just stepping outside. Be right back."

Shane left before she could question him further. Once he slipped out of the front door he removed his cell phone. He dialed home first. "Mom?"

"Where the hell are you? Where?"

"Calm down."

"Shane, they took Scotty. I got a call from Phyllis. She said two men snatched him off the streets. Then your father calls. You saw him? Why? Shane? What are you into? Rock said that you were to go see Barbara of all people... that crazy bitch can't be trusted! Does Ian know you saw your father? Shane? Is that why they took Scotty?"

Shane shook his head ruefully and fumed. "Are you sure Higgins has Scotty?"

Little could be understood over his mother's babble and tears.

An alarmingly cold rush of anger, mixed with dread, hit him full force. He paced the short sidewalk. Raelynn said they had time. Well time was up, Higgins must have found out that Mickey was dead. Dammit he should have known better. If Ian picked up Scotty then it's game over.

"Mom! Listen to me. How long since Scotty went missing?"

"Your father swore he'd keep you out of this Shane. Then he calls here and wants me to send you right back in. I knew things were bad between us when you left. I knew it. But you can't get involved with Rock. He doesn't have your best interest at heart, and, and he hates me. He blames me Shane. Now he will take you away from me. I can't…You can't."

"When did they take Scotty?"

"Last night."

"Shit! Shit!" Shane ended the call. He worried over who to trust next. Maybe Cass could help? Shane's head lifted, as did his gaze when the slow purr of a motorcycle engine drew closer. A man drove up on a bike to the house next door. A night ride was something Shane often did. The bike's chrome gleamed under the dim streetlights. He couldn't believe his luck. He watched the man rise from the bike seat and remove his helmet and then approached. "Hey man, I got a question for you?"

The guy looked back at Shane, curious. Before he could reply Shane delivered one hard punch that knocked him flat. He grabbed the keys to the bike and hopped on. He looked over to the house and considered the ramifications of his actions. What would become of the trust he and Raelynn shared? Shane fired up the bike and again made peace with who he was and wasn't. Either way, things would end for him and Rae. At the very least he could save his cousin's life before he tossed his.

Raelynn rose from the sofa. Shane hadn't returned from his call after ten minutes. She knew he was just outside of the door, but still something gnawed at her.

"Raelynn!" Andrea called from the basement.

She glanced back toward the basement door. Raelynn opted to check on Andrea instead of Shane. She bounded down the carpeted steps into the darkly lit basement, careful of the shadowy obstacles barely defined under the red glow of the developer's light. Her friend had developed several pictures that were drying. Raelynn stepped forward and examined them. The first pictures were of a gathering of men. One of them in particular had to be Ian Higgins; one of the others who looked a bit more somber had to be a younger Rock Lafferty.

"We're almost done. You got about thirty shots here. Thought you and that hottie of yours would like to see them as they developed."

"He's not my hottie."

"No he's your fuck-buddy." Andrea sang. "What kind of agent are you, screwing your suspect?"

When Raelynn didn't answer Andrea looked up. It must have been on her face: shame, regret, anger. Andrea's playful smile died. "Sorry girl. You know I can be an ass. It came out wrong."

"It's a fair question. One I've asked myself over and over." Raelynn paced away. "I've broken every rule I learned in the Academy, and it wasn't because of Shane. It's me."

"You? You're great at what you do. Hell Olivia and I were just talking the other day about how proud we are for you."

Raelynn sighed. "Yes I know. Everyone's proud, you're proud, my dad's proud, my Section Chief was so proud he assigned me to a task force that could make my career. And what do I do? Sabotage it. I don't know. I have to wonder what's going on with me."

Andrea shuffled over. She put her hand to Raelynn's cheek. "You have a heart girl, and you use it. That makes you the best kind of agent. Besides, I'm not into white boys, but that one upstairs could definitely convince me. He's cute."

Raelynn laughed.

Andrea went back to her developer table. The urge to rage against her mistakes subsided. Sharing who Shane was had been her mild attempt to tame Andrea—and a reaction of instant jealousy over how she flirted with him in her face. She hadn't anticipated the self-reflection it brought forward. For the first time she admitted aloud that her crusade to be the best federal agent wasn't just about career advancement. She felt obligated in some way to make her father's dreams realized. Raelynn set aside those questions. She studied the image of the men in the photo. She wondered whose hand Ian shook.

"Holy mother of God!" Andrea gasped.

"What?" Raelynn turned.

Andrea stepped back from the processing tray. "Look."

Raelynn had to move closer to see the image floating in the solution. It was a clear shot of Ian Higgins with a gun pressed to the back of the head of a man kneeling. "The smoking gun? Finish developing the rest of this film."

"What the hell is this Raelynn? What am I going to see next?"

Andrea asked, her voice faltering, revealing her fear.

"Don't know. But I need your help. Just do it okay? Please."

Andrea looked back to the tray and then to Raelynn. "Okay."

The doorbell chimed above them. Raelynn frowned. "Why is Shane ringing the doorbell?" she hurried up the stairs. She could see the flashing police lights through the front windows of the house. Raelynn's heart dropped. She had only called one person to tell them where she and Shane were. The only person she could trust. "No Andy, you wouldn't." She rushed the door and flung it open. Andy O'Brien, her partner since she graduated Quantico, turned with a folder in his hand. A young man with brown shaggy hair and a short stocky build, Andy had been a faithful friend and colleague from the first day they met. She trusted him.

Raelynn's gaze shifted past his wan smile to the two officers walking away. She searched for an image of Shane being loaded to the back of a police car. Instead she saw EMT's gathered on Andrea's neighbor's lawn. A man in a motorcycle jacket received medical attention on the lawn. Shane was gone.

"What the hell happened?"

"You tell me." Andy walked in. Raelynn's heart began to race as her mind puzzled through Shane's disappearance. The scene made no sense. "Did you see him?"

"No, but your friend's neighbor did. He attacked him and stole his bike."

"No, Shane wouldn't do that."

Andy looked at her with disgust. Raelynn closed the door. "I can explain."

"Explain? How many times have we talked about a break like this, the chance of our careers? A joint task force with the ATF, and they put you front and center in the investigation first? My ego could handle it Raelynn. Why? Because you're smart, sharp, and you would bust your ass for the opportunity. Now? Greaves and Director Harvey say you've put the entire investigation in jeopardy. Raelynn they could report you to the Office of the Inspector General. You need to come in with me now and clear this up."

Raelynn sighed. "You don't understand."

"No? Then help me? Why the hell is Melissa Harvey gunning for you? Orders are to bring you in. And I'm telling you Raelynn, the ATF is blaming us for this." He shook the folder at her. "I had to throw those cops outside off your scent. That thug-boyfriend of yours attacked a man, and stole a bike right outside this door and you didn't even know!"

"Boyfriend?" Raelynn frowned.

"Everyone knows Raelynn. Agent Reyes returned to the office from Atlanta furious. He said you ditched him twice. One check and they found out you were held up with Shane Lafferty in a hotel. A hotel! You knew they'd trace your cards, track you. What is going on in your head?"

"You know me. I wouldn't take these chances if um, I, um, didn't have a plan. That's why I called you. Shane isn't our target. He's the key. I needed time to work him, not the way you think. We aren't intimately involved." She lied. She hated to hear the lie escape her lips, but she was losing credibility with the only man left who could help her. "I…"

"Read this."

He handed her a folder.

She accepted it. "What's this?"

"The truth about this Shane character that you're trying so desperately to save."

Raelynn looked up at Andy and then to the folder in her hand. She stepped back, and lowered to the seat behind her. When she opened the folder she found an incident report from local police. A hit and run. The victim was hospitalized for two months then confined to a wheel chair for the rest of her young life.

"Her name is Carla Mathews. Two years ago she and some friends left a party thrown in Shane's honor. When they crossed the street a car ran through the red light. That car hit her, sent her several feet in the air before it drove over her legs and crushed them. Witnesses said the car didn't even brake, but they were able to provide the license plate number. Since the accident, that information has been purged from the file. The witnesses who said they saw the car, are now all scattered throughout the country with permanent cases of amnesia. Carla Mathews, received a generous donation of money from Ian Higgins and never spoke of the incident. That folder is one of the many the ATF have on the men in this case."

"Why are you giving it to me?"

"Because the driver was Shane Lafferty."

Raelynn frowned. "It doesn't say…."

"The license plate was to his car. The cover-up went down a few days before his big boxing match. It's the reason he threw the fight and left town. To pay back the debt for the cover-up. He nearly killed that girl and he had Ian Higgins bury the truth. Now you tell me again Raelynn, is this guy really worth your career?"

CHAPTER SEVENTEEN

Shane parked at the back of Gladiators. He made sure to avoid the main roads, and took the side streets. Thankfully the late hour concealed him. He expected to find the gym empty with Cass in the back doing his books. Instead the gym bustled with activity.

Why?

Something had to be up. Shane chuckled. He'd almost forgotten about his upcoming match. In a matter of twenty-four hours, Raelynn had him forgetting his dream and looking forward to prison. It was madness. He pulled the hood out from under his leather jacket and flipped it over his baseball cap. Any unseen surveillance would think of him as nothing more than one of Cass's boys.

"Wsup Shane?" Skeet asked once he passed. "We were looking for you yesterday. Cass was all worked up. You missed your press conference."

Shane nodded but kept going. Danny sparred in the ring with some young punk Shane didn't know. Shane's gaze lifted and locked with Danny's. His sparring partner delivered a stunning blow that threw him into the ropes. Danny continued to stare at Shane as he passed him by. The accusation in his eyes made Shane's blood run cold. Did they really know Mickey was dead? If they did then Scotty's chances of survival were slim.

Quick and determined he hurried his steps. Cass wasn't in the gym, possibly he'd been held up in the back of his office. He knew Shane would return. Shane had sworn he'd come after wrestling Barbara's address from him.

When Shane crossed through the shifting double doors to the back he stopped in the hall. Big Al looked up. The bastard appeared to be waiting for someone—possibly him. A dark sneer was tattooed to his face. Shane could run, but there really would be no need. The boys in the gym would side with Al and stop him before he reached the door. And Al wasn't opposed to shooting him in the back rather than bothering to give chase.

"Well Shaney, welcome back. Been waiting for you."

"Where's Cass?"

"Cass shouldn't be your concern. I am. You coming with me Shaney, now." Big Al withdrew his gun from the inside of his holster tucked under his jacket. Shane dropped his hands in his front pockets trying to appear less intimidated. He watched Al's approach. His mind calculated the options again for Scotty's rescue. He came up short. So he decided not to think it through. As soon as Al stopped within striking distance Shane delivered the hardest punch of his career, directly to the tall man's jaw. Stunned the six foot six giant dropped the weapon in his hand. Shane kicked Al in the scrotum, then punched him hard again in the head, leveling him to the floor. Out cold, Al lay motionless, face down. Shane panted hard, rage, fear and dread left him wild with adrenaline. He lifted his hand and stared at the blood on his knuckles. Now what should he do? He knelt and picked up the weapon. Stepping over Al he headed for Cass's office. He found it empty. "Shit." Shane ran for the door.

**

"This can't be true." Raelynn stammered. She felt sick. Images of her father's torment as he went through recovery swarmed her. She recalled the doctor's words when he shared the depressing news with her and her mom that her father would never walk again, and the years of therapy that followed. "Shane didn't do this. There's another explanation."

"I came here to warn you and help you. We can fix this. Bring him in together and tell Director Greaves he took you hostage. It's your word against his. Do some damage control Raelynn before it's too late. You might walk away with a brief suspension. If we do it the right way."

Stunned Raelynn couldn't breathe. She stared at the image of the woman whose life was lost because of Shane's reckless thoughtlessness and felt sadness swell deep inside of her. *He'd been playing her all along.* She slammed the folder shut. "No. I won't lie, become like him." She mumbled.

"What? Of course you will lie and get the hell out of this mess before it's too late." Andy warned.

"Too late? I think it already is Andy. I plan to see this through."

"But..."

Andrea entered the room from behind Raelynn. She only knew

of her presence by the curious look on her partner's face. She turned to find Andrea, actually pale and visibly shaken. Raelynn stood. "What is it?"

Andrea dried her hands and shook her head. "Nasty pictures. Men being murdered."

"What pictures?" Andy asked.

Raelynn forced a patient tone to her voice. "Stay right here. Show me." She said to her friend and marched back downstairs to the basement. The roll of film had been processed. Raelynn slowly walked the line of a murder scene. Rock Lafferty stood to the left of the scene, but never once did he draw a weapon. The men executed were done so by Ian Higgins's hand, in some macabre ritual. It appeared as if those gathered watched in appreciation. Raelynn tried to focus on the faces of the men present. One of them struck her as familiar, and when she finally recognized the man her heart sank. "So this is what you found out Shane? This is why you ran from here?"

"It's disgusting. Those poor men. Who the hell takes pictures of a murder?" Andrea mumbled.

"Are these okay? Can I take them?"

Andrea walked over and nodded. She took the pictures and wiped each with a dry cloth and then tucked them in an envelope.

"I need the negatives."

Andrea didn't question her. Raelynn slipped the plastic sleeve of negatives in her pocket. She smiled wanly at her friend. "Thanks, for everything."

"Are you in trouble Raelynn? Are you investigating these men?"

"Not anymore. After this afternoon it's not my case, hell probably not even my job. I'll take care of myself."

"Raelynn wait." Andrea stopped in front of her. "I know you're a federal agent and what you do is dangerous. But girl, not until I looked at those pictures did I understand how serious your job is. Please be careful. I'm scared for you."

She embraced her friend. The hurt over Shane's lies and his abandonment of their deal still burned hot in her chest. Raelynn suppressed the urge to say so. Her eyes watered behind her shut lids, she blinked away the misty tears. "I'll be fine. I'll call you tonight when this is all over."

She bounded back up the stairs. Andy paced a tight circle in the middle of the floor. He looked up when she approached. She had one envelope in her hand. The negatives were buried deep in her jacket pocket. "You were right Andy. I lost my way. Now I need your help partner. Take these."

Andy accepted the envelope. "What is it?"

"The key to your promotion. You deserve an assignment that'll get you out from behind the desk. Take these photos in and you will be front and center on this investigation. Make sure you put them in the hands of Greaves to present to Director Harvey."

"Don't trust the ATF, huh?" Andy chuckled.

"I trust Melissa Harvey to do exactly what she does."

"What are these photos?"

"The smoking gun."

"Literally." Andrea mumbled, reminding them she too was in the room. Raelynn's gaze slipped her way and she saw how her friend visibly shivered.

"It will incriminate Ian Higgins and take down the ITZ. I just need you to do me a favor."

Andy nodded.

"Give me a twenty minute head start before you report me. Tell them I tried to make contact with you, and send them to Ian Higgins's office. Tell them that you got a tip that the ITZ will have a buy going down early, and I'm trying to go rogue and do the bust alone. Send as many reinforcements as you can, make a big spectacle of this Andy. I need our presence to be revealed."

"What are you doing Raelynn?" Andy's brow furrowed.

Raelynn walked toward the door. "Ending this charade. Time that the bad boys are made to pay."

"Alone? Raelynn wait."

She glanced back. "I need a chance to redeem myself. I trusted Shane, like you said he wasn't worth it. Now I've got to restore a bit of my dignity and bring a little justice too. Believe me, if this goes down the way I plan it we will both walk away with what we need." She mumbled. She knew where Shane had run off to. The stakes were high. Shane had left her no other choice.

**

Shane heard voices. Two distinct voices barked angrily at each other. He approached the doors to Ian Higgins's office with the gun in his hand. Without Al to stand guard, Ian's men were scattered and not the least bit ruffled by Shane's appearance. Ian Higgins had to remain a legit businessman to others, so he didn't keep armed men at his place of business. No one would stop him from carrying out what he planned. But the voice sharply speaking beyond the door rang familiar. It stopped Shane cold.

"I'm telling you Shane had nothing to do with the Feds killing Mickey." Cass insisted.

"You've said that twice, but I know differently. My contacts confirmed it. Shane's negotiating with the Feds as we speak. My contacts are never wrong. I know you care for the kid Cass but it's time to let him go. I don't need a boxing champion, I'm done with the headache."

"It's Rock's boy Ian. He deserves to be heard out. Taking Scotty was a good move. Shane will come out of hiding like he always does. When he does, we hear him out. Plus Rock saved us all from prison. He gave his life and you got all the power. All he wanted was for us to look after Shane."

Ian laughed. "Who said I took Scotty? The runt is a coward, and he's useless."

"I know you took Scotty. I'm trying to keep this in perspective."

"Are you seriously going to stand here and try to be some moral voice of reason? Cass I know you mentor those kids, but come the fuck on. You and I know you are no friend to Rock Lafferty."

Shane frowned. His hand slowly turned on the cool steel of the doorknob and he eased the door open a crack. Cass stood to the side of Higgins's desk. He nearly threw the door open wide to challenge Ian on the facts when Cass spoke again.

"I believed you when you said that we needed to stand strong, to align with the ITZ. I did what I did for boys like Shane. Tipping those cops off to Rock disposing of the bodies of the Lithuanians had been necessary. Rock wanted to split Southie with those scumbags, stop all the violence. He had turned soft."

"No. Rock never turned soft. You did Cass. For pussy. You were jealous of Rock, and you were fucking his wife. All these years you and that drunk bitch hid your little affair from Shane, and blamed me. Hell Rock isn't stupid. I'm sure down in that penitentiary he figured out who was really banging Margene. That it was you Cass, and when I'm done with your pet boxing boy he will know the truth. What you and his mother did to his father to cover your affair."

Shane tossed the door open with a raised gun. Both men looked up at his sudden arrival. "Is it true? Did you set my father up?" he asked Cass.

Ian rocked back in his chair amused. He wasn't the least bit concerned over the weapon in Shane's hand. "Is it true?"

"Let me explain son."

"You and Margene? You set up my father?"

"Your mother had nothing to do with it." Cass said. "Yes, we had an affair, but she didn't know what I would be forced to do."

Ian clapped and laughed. "Good one Cass. You expect Shane to believe you were forced to set up the man whose wife you banged?"

Cass stepped forward. "Those times were different. The Lithuanians were moving in and taking over. The ITZ wanted a show of force and your father didn't. We were divided. It goes against our core Shane. It's a brotherhood and an honor to be a member." Cass pointed a chubby finger at the amused mob boss turned businessman. "Ian changed it. He forced my hand, he wanted to take everything your father and I built. He invited The Brotherhood from Ireland to watch him execute the Lithuanians.

The ITZ demands loyalty and a show of power, Ian had them thinking we were weakened by Rock. We all had to prove our commitment to the cause. Once it was done, your father was chosen to do away with the bodies. The power had shifted." Cass rushed out in a single breath.

"The ITZ thought centralized leadership here and in Chicago would draw in more members. Expand our territory; help with unloading the guns here out of Ireland. It meant a different kind of leadership. Rock was mostly brawn and muscle; I was a follower not a leader. Ian could talk his way out of anything, and he convinced the ITZ to do Rock in. They forced me to set him up to take the fall for the whole thing."

"Oh quit your lying and bellyaching Cass." Ian switched his gaze to Shane. "I never wanted Rock gone. Rock had balls. He'd done a lot to build Southie, to make us the men we are today. Rock made the tough calls. He insisted we didn't have a single leader Shane, makes one man a target if we did. It was a smart way for us to co-lead then.

"But things had to change. We were only soldiers for The Brotherhood then, and we needed a leader. Rock understood these things the night the Lithuanians were made to pay. He stepped aside and let me lead, he wanted to leave it all behind to be a family man, take care of you and your mother. But your surrogate father here wanted something else. He wanted your mother. I have to admit

Margene was a nice piece of ass back in the day. But she was too self destructive for my taste. Cass could never take her from Rock, so he took Rock from her. He called the cops and tipped them off to your father disposing of the bodies. Your old man used to say 'give a man a hundred…"

"And he'll take a hundred more." Shane finally tore his gaze from Cass to Ian. However, he never lowered the weapon. His finger itched to pull the trigger.

"Exactly. So Rock chose family over The Brotherhood and I took a hundred more. He still has influence you know? He's not a rat. What are you Shane?"

"Shut up!" Shane snarled.

When Shane didn't lower the gun or respond Ian smirked. "Your father made the ultimate sacrifice. Thing is, Cass didn't get his reward. Stupid broad started drinking even more. Her guilt I suppose. So Cass focused on making it up to you. Training you, being a father to you, all to assuage his guilt. I'm not the man who destroyed your family son, Cass is."

"Shane…" Cass started.

"Shut up! You fucking lying bastard!" He gripped the gun with both hands that shook from the wrist down. Tears streaked down his face. He would have to kill the man he considered a father. The mere idea of it made him sick to his stomach with rage, and regret. "Fucking lying bastard!"

"Put the weapon down Shane!" Raelynn said from behind him.

The men looked surprised at her arrival. Shane felt the barrel of her gun to the back of his skull. "Do it. Now. And gentlemen I suggest you don't move."

"What are you doing here Rae?" Shane stammered.

"Now!" She ordered.

Ian chuckled. "Sweetheart, I heard about you. At last we meet. Who says the Feds are never around when you need them?"

"In ten minutes this place will be surrounded. There is no walking out of here. Shane, I won't tell you again. Drop the gun."

"Rae, leave!"

"Do as I said!" she released the safety on the gun. He heard the determined resolve in her voice. For a brief second he didn't think she'd hesitate to pull the trigger. He glared at Cass who stood so still it didn't even look like he was breathing. His gaze switched to Ian. "Where's Scotty?"

Ian chuckled. "Again with Scotty? I tell you, your stand in daddy here put your old man behind bars, and you want to know where that sniveling piece of shit Scotty is? You disappoint me Shane."

Shane turned the gun on the mobster. "I'm dead either way Ian. You and I both know it. Tell me where my cousin is or I will pull this trigger."

"No you won't!" Raelynn shouted behind him. He ignored her and maintained Ian's stare.

The truth flashed in Ian's dark sneer. *Scotty was dead.* Shane grimaced and almost pulled the trigger when everything went dark.

CHAPTER EIGHTEEN

Raelynn stood over Shane. She'd hit him hard to the back of the head with her gun. He dropped instantly. She raised the gun to the men before her. "Don't move. Don't make a fucking move."

In rushed the agents she knew Andy would bring, weapons drawn. Ian Higgins rose, his face hard as stone, his attire immaculate. He narrowed his gaze on Raelynn, then lowered it to Shane before he dismissed them both when an agent approached and began to read him his rights. He looked almost bored with the routine, as he and Cass were both lead out. Raelynn lowered to Shane. More federal agents in bullet proof vests swarmed inside.

"Is he dead?" Andy asked.

"No. He needs medical attention, I hit him. I had no choice. I didn't mean to hurt him." Raelynn fumbled around her explanation. She frowned when her fingers touched the sticky trace of blood to the back of Shane's head. Did she hurt him? He'd already suffered one head blow, what damage would the second one have caused?

She flinched when an agent cuffed him, and Shane groaned

through regaining consciousness. The men handling him roughly brought him upright to his feet. Raelynn nearly objected, but she looked up into the eyes of Director Melissa Harvey as she stepped in with Director Greaves. Ian gave her a wink when he passed her in handcuffs, mouthing the words: be seeing you soon. Director Harvey caught his threat. The rage on her face made Raelynn's stomach sour. She stepped aside while two men in FBI jackets half carried, half dragged Shane out the open door.

"So, where are the Irish?" Director Harvey asked.

"I can explain, ma'am." Raelynn began.

"Don't bother Agent, save it for the O.I.G. You are to report back to the bureau and wait to hear from your unit chief. Agent O'Brien, Reyes, can you gentlemen make sure Agent Traylor finds her way. She has a habit of not following rules."

Raelynn holstered her gun and walked out. When she crossed out of the restaurant into the street she looked up to see Shane being placed in the back of an unmarked car. His gaze briefly lifted her way, then shifted away. Raelynn swallowed her bitter resentment and climbed into the dark SUV with her escorts.

Two Hours later—

"Raelynn?" Andy opened the door to the room where she was being detained. Since she arrived at the bureau she was treated no better than the criminals she had sworn to bring down. In fact she had been shoved aside in a room to await her fate. The time alone had been quite sobering. The bureaucracy she'd face and possible suspension for her actions weren't her first concern. Shane had deceived her, she told him about her father and still he said nothing about Carla Mathews.

"Two things," Andy walked inside and closed the door. "One, they've already released Ian Higgins."

"What?" Raelynn asked, standing. "That's not possible. Did you give Harvey the pictures?"

Andy nodded.

"I don't understand. Why did she release him?"

"ATF is really pissed about the missed opportunity with the Irish. Their entire case was built on that bust Raelynn. I'm not sure, but I get the feeling they are going to pass the bank robbery over to us, and the only arrest we have on the books for that is for Shane Lafferty and his cousin. I'm sorry."

Raelynn hoped things wouldn't go south, but she suspected it might. "You said two things?"

"Before you face the firing squad I thought you should be granted a visitor. She's pretty insistent on speaking with you. Keeps calling you the 'black Fed' who took her son."

Raelynn frowned. "Who?"

"I believe her name is Margene Lafferty, Shane's mother. I got her waiting. Do you want to talk to her?"

Raelynn released an amused chuckle. "You're kidding right? In an hour my career is about to end and you want to know if I want to commiserate with Shane Lafferty's mother?"

Andy stepped over to her. "I trust you Rae. There's a reason you went to the lengths you did to help him. And I get the feeling that you aren't about to roll over and take a spanking from Melissa Harvey. This Lafferty woman might give you some additional information to use. It can't hurt. That's why I made sure you got a crack at her first."

Raelynn bit down on her bottom lip until her teeth sunk into the tender flesh. "Fine. Where did you stick her?"

"A3."

She touched Andy's arm, "Thanks, for everything."

"It's not over until it's over. Right?" Andy said.

Raelynn doubted her smile convinced him, but she made the effort anyway. Then she walked out and quickly entered the conference room where Shane's mother waited without being seen. The office buzzed with activity so it wasn't too hard.

A very distraught woman sat on the edge of a brown leather chair facing away from the office window. Her eyes lifted and fixed on Raelynn. They were red rimmed and weepy. Her cheeks were slick with fresh tears. She looked haggard, but Raelynn could tell beneath her scruffy appearance she had once been a beautiful woman. The woman wiped away the trace of tears and stood, trying to fix her ill-fitted dress. She was a foot shorter than Raelynn and so thin she would almost be considered bony. Her dress was wrinkled and her shoes were worn over. She really looked a state.

"Are you her? The agent Rock said was with Shane? Are you?"

"I am. My name is…"

"I don't care! I'm here to confess."

Raelynn double blinked. "You what?"

"I'm here to confess. My boy is innocent. He had nothing to do with Ian Higgins, the Irish mob, none of it. He only got involved with those people because of me."

"Are you aware of what Shane is charged with?" Raelynn

pressed.

"Don't matter. I'm here to confess. The only crime you should care about is the one I did. Two years ago Shane had a party, Ian and Cass threw it at Gladiators. It was to celebrate his match. Go ahead check it out. The party is documented. Celebrities came."

"Mrs. Lafferty…."

"Listen to me dammit! I… I got into an argument with Cass. Never mind why. I just did. And when I get upset, I drink. I just do. I started drinking and I didn't stop. I knew it would ruin Shane's party but I didn't care. And when I couldn't stand being there, seeing Cass and Ian and knowing what they'd done, I tried to leave. Shane saw me. He caught up with me and we fought."

"I ran from him, I had his keys. He tried to get me to get out of the car. I wouldn't. So he got in the passenger side. We argued. He told me to pull over, even tried to take the wheel. I was upset. Really upset. I don't know, why but I drove faster. I ran a red light and I hit that poor girl. Ran over her I did. And I didn't stop. Shane got control of the car and he took the blame for me. Ian made that go away. Shane learned the woman would never walk again. It broke him, what we done. It broke my baby, so he left. He should have stayed gone."

Raelynn listened in shock. She had blamed and convicted Shane in her heart for this accident, and all the while he was protecting his mother. "Your confession doesn't matter. Shane isn't charged with the hit and run. He's charged with armed robbery."

"No. Not my Shane. He's a good boy. Ian did it. He set him up."

"The way Cass, Shane's manager set up his father?" Raelynn

asked. Margene froze. She doubled back from the accusation. Finally she found her voice and spoke. "That's a lie. An Ian Higgins lie. Arrest me, but let Shane go."

"I can't." Raelynn turned for the door.

"You heartless bitch!" Margene shouted to her back.

Raelynn froze. "What did you call me?"

Margene wiped the snot from her nose. "I called you a bitch."

Raelynn glared. "You have a lot of nerve. Your son's life is in the toilet because you couldn't put the bottle down long enough to be a mother! Shane knows you set up his father with his trainer Cass. My guess is Rock Lafferty does too."

"Not true!"

"Shane would rather go to prison than spend another day being your nurse maid. Do him a favor and disappear."

"How dare you!"

Raelynn didn't bother to reply. She could get nothing useful from that woman. It was time she fought back with the only weapon she had. Raelynn marched straight to her Director's office. She opened the door without knocking. Just as she suspected Melissa Harvey was there, along with her Section Chief. They looked up, a bit annoyed at her arrival.

"Excuse me sir, I'd like to be heard."

"Agent Traylor, we will send for you when we are ready." Commander Greaves warned in a disapproving tone.

"This can't wait."

Melissa smiled. "Then by all means come in. Gentlemen I think it's fine that we speak with her now. Please," the Director gestured to the empty sofa seats. "Have a seat Raelynn."

Raelynn swallowed her nervousness. She didn't sit. She faced them all. "I'd like to know what will be done with Shane Lafferty?"

Harvey looked at Raelynn's superiors; Elliot Greaves nodded for her to share the news. "He's going to prison, where he belongs."

"And Ian Higgins?" Raelynn pressed.

Harvey narrowed her eyes. "That investigation is still ongoing."

"I'm told you cut him loose." Raelynn said.

The Director stepped closer. "I did, and do you know why Agent?" She glowered. "Because thanks to you an investigation that is fifteen years in the making collapsed today. Ian Higgins and the Irish won't be meeting. The ITZ has shut down the sell. It will take us another decade to gain the intelligence we've lost. Maybe even longer to close this case."

"I provided you proof that Higgins killed the men Rock Lafferty had been convicted of murdering. Irrefutable proof. What about that?" Raelynn asked.

The Director laughed. "What about it? We didn't ask for it, and we don't need it! Besides, we always knew that Higgins killed the Lithuanians. What we need is evidence against those Irish loyalist scumbags trafficking guns across our borders. I understand you're a rookie, but even you know how this plays out."

"Melissa." Greaves interrupted.

"Speak to your agent. She's not an idiot. Tell her how this works!"

"No." Raelynn said firmly. "I will tell you how this works. Shane Lafferty gets the deal I offered. He'll testify after he's put in witness protection."

"Testify? Or what?" Melissa scoffed.

"Or those images you've suppressed will leak to the press. No disrespect ma'am, but you're making a bad call here. I don't have the negatives. Shane does. He won't sit on them. He'll use it to bargain with if we don't give him something else." Raelynn swallowed another dose of courage to keep her voice from wavering. "Shane and his father can give you the ITZ. They can connect the dots all the way to Ireland, and all they want is for you to give them justice with Ian Higgins. Ma'am, it's the best plan."

Melissa sneered. "Are you trying to hustle me Agent?"

"That's enough Harvey."

"She...."

"Enough." Elliot Greaves said. He rose from behind his desk. "We don't have a case without the Lafferty's. Those images leak and you will lose the Irish in this. The money and man-hours spent on the investigation can't go down the tubes. We have an opportunity here. I think Traylor has given us more than your fifteen years of intelligence has. Even your informant is dead. Without his testimony how exactly do you think we can pin the robbery on Lafferty? He doesn't know it yet, but by the time he lawyers up he will. We need to act now."

Raelynn secretly released a deep breath of relief. She physically relaxed. When she returned her gaze to Melissa Harvey she didn't see as much distrust as she did before. But it remained. Harvey stepped forward. "Fine Elliot. But Agent Traylor should be suspended from this case, and the bureau for her insubordination."

"How was I insubordinate? I worked a lead, just as I was told.

You gave me forty-eight hours and I..."

"We have a dead informant, and a criminal with inside knowledge of our investigation. At the very least we need to be sure exactly how far you went to 'work a lead'."

Raelynn shifted her gaze to her Section Chief, then to Commander Greaves. "Shane won't listen to anyone but me. Let me at least talk to him. Make sure he cooperates. Then, discipline me sir, if you must. Give me a chance to correct my mistakes."

The silent stand off lasted longer than she would have preferred.

"Make it clear to him that we need his testimony and his father's or no deal."

"And his cousin sir? He's a witness too, and useful." Raelynn pushed. "My partner said, you have his cousin in custody."

Greaves smiled. "Go ahead Traylor. See it through."

"Yes sir."

Shane's head felt as if it been stuffed with rocks. He literally had to rest his face in his palms to keep his head up. Everything he believed about the people he loved burned in flames. Years of manipulations by his mentor left him weak and humiliated. He heard the lock on the door to his cell disengage and didn't bother to look up. Wherever they took him next didn't matter. He just didn't want to exist.

"Shane?"

Slowly his face lifted from his palms. He blinked and his vision cleared.

"Have you had medical attention?" Raelynn asked.

He lowered his gaze to the floor. The last person he wanted to see was Raelynn, though he supposed she'd come eventually for her pound of flesh too. Shane decided to make it easy for her. "Tell them I will confess."

"Be quiet Shane." Raelynn said sternly. "Not another word until your attorney arrives."

He lifted his gaze.

Raelynn wiped her hands down her sides and approached him. She looked nervous. Her agitation stressed him. He couldn't bear it.

"Listen to me. We can make you a deal. But first I've asked that you get some medical attention. You need to see a doctor."

"I'm no rat."

"Oh please. Spare me the honor amongst thugs crap. Everyone in your life has lied to you and now you want to take the high road? I'm sick of the martyr routine Shane. First your mom, then your cousin, then your mom again. You look for excuses not to move on."

"You don't know me!"

"I know enough. You will take this deal dammit. I've lost too much and so have you to walk away now. You testify, along with your father, on everything you know about the ITZ. My bosses will put you in the Witness Protection Program along with your cousin."

Shane frowned. The action caused his face to hurt.

Raelynn nodded.

"Scotty's dead."

"No Shane, we have him. They picked him up, not Ian Higgins. If you hadn't of run out on me I would have told you."

Shane sat upright from his slouch. He looked Raelynn over to try to understand the trick. "Something's different. Why are you helping me? Aren't you pissed at me for dragging you into this?"

Raelynn sighed. "I found out about the accident. The hit and run. You should have told me! That poor woman is in a wheelchair and you made it all go away for your mother."

"And you hate me because I'm like the criminal who put your father in a wheelchair, right?"

"Wrong. You're broken. I don't agree with what you've done and who you were. But I… I think you've paid enough. Take the deal Shane. Talk to your father again and make sure he gives the F.B.I the information they need. Do it Shane, and then get a fresh start."

"Will I ever see you again Rae?"

She smiled sadly. "No. This is goodbye. I'm sorry. I am."

"Yeah. Me too. I've made a lot of mistakes Rae, but you and I. I think it's the only thing I've done right. Do you understand?"

She nodded. "I think I do."

She looked as if she would touch him but stopped herself. She backed away from him and turned for the door.

"Rae?"

"Yes?" she said not looking back.

"Never mind."

She nodded and left him. Shane lowered back on the bunk in his cell. He closed his eyes. "Never mind."

CHAPTER NINETEEN

Six months later

"Mom, how is he?" Raelynn stood; her hand went to her belly. She searched the face of the doctor and her mother. The grief in her mother's eyes ripped at her heart. Raelynn struggled not to fall apart, so she returned her focus to the doctor. "How is my father?"

"No Change. The Pneumonia has spread through his lungs. We have to wait to see if he responds to the treatment. If not, well his immune system is pretty weak."

"I can't... I can't..." Her mother wailed. Raelynn was at her side in a flash. She helped her mother sit and tried again to keep from crying herself.

The doctor looked at them with sympathy. "He's a strong man, he could pull out of this."

"Thank you doctor." Raelynn said sadly.

The doctor walked off. Raelynn held her mother until her tears stopped, but her mom continued to cling to her. She sat in the hospital hall watching the nurses and orderlies pass them by. She never felt so helpless. When she got the call that her father had been taken into the hospital for respiratory problems, she thought it treatable. Now a diagnosis of Pneumonia proved how fragile her father's life could be. A bought of déjà vu hit her full force. She could vividly remember the terror and fear when she and her mother sat in the same hospital praying for a miracle after his shooting. Why would God send them here again?

"Raelynn," her mother sniffed. "You okay, is the baby okay?"

"Yes Ma. We're fine."

"No sweetheart," her mother's eyes lowered to her bulge. She could see the pain and confusion in her stare. Raelynn couldn't bring herself to share the details of the baby's conception and the way she deceived her parents. She had been a coward.

"When were you going to tell us?"

"I had planned to come home for Christmas, before Dad got sick. I um, planned to move home maybe."

"Move? But your job?"

"I quit three months ago. Mom it's a long story. I'm sorry."

"Hush, hush baby, we can talk about it tonight." Her mother cupped her face and kissed her forehead. "Your daddy is going to need us both to be strong."

Raelynn nodded. "I um, need to get some air. Can I get you something?"

"No. I'll wait in Phillip's room." Her mother said and rose sadly. Raelynn helped steady her on her feet. Philip Traylor was the lifeblood of their family. If he died, Raelynn knew her mother wouldn't be the same. She watched her go then forced her legs to move. Before long she found herself outside of the hospital pacing away from the emergency doors, desperate for space and the will to breathe. The panic consuming her made all of it seem impossible.

"Raelynn? That you?"

She paused. Turning she saw Michael Thomas approaching her. He wore his khaki brown sheriff uniform and a broad brim sheriff's hat on his head. He gave her that lazy smile that made her melt back in high school. He had the shiniest blue eyes that always captured the one looking into them and calmed them. His smile soon faded at the sight of her belly.

"How's the Chief?" Michael stammered, unable to lift his eyes from her girth. He always called her father 'Chief' though he was no more than a patrol officer before the shooting.

Raelynn forced a smile. "Not so good. Pneumonia."

"I'm sorry sweetheart." He said extending his arm.

It felt natural for Raelynn to drift into his arms. She held him and released her tears, a shocking action that unleashed a flood of painful regret. It had been a miserable six months.

The pregnancy was the only bright spot in her life. For three of the months she sat on the sidelines and watched the trial and conviction of Ian Higgins and the other men tied to the ITZ. She wanted to tell Shane about the baby, but she could never get close enough. She'd only glimpsed Shane twice and once when he was on the stand.

The distance between them could not be breeched. She ached so deeply for him she almost resigned from the FBI. Work however was her saving grace. Her suspension lasted for a total of 14 days, and then she again was back behind her desk. She concealed her pregnancy from her superiors, trying to think of the best way to announce it. A kid had never been part of the bargain. She and Shane had been so careful. There was no explaining her pregnancy. So she took the coward's way out and asked for a leave. The Director seemed eager to give it to her. Three months later she resigned and Shane was gone. Now her father's illness made all her inner conflicts surface.

"Hey? You okay?" Michael asked.

She lifted her head and smiled into his kind eyes. "I don't think so."

"How about something to eat? You can tell me all about it."

"Okay."

Raelynn walked with him, her arm around his waist. Michael had always been easy to talk to, and she desperately needed the chance to talk to someone right now.

Battle Creek, Minnesota –

"Shane! Shane!"

Shane looked up from his chores. He walked out of the stall with the shovel in his hands. Scotty running in and yelling his name stirred the horses. He frowned. The stench of his sweat from hard labor and manure clogged his nostrils. He didn't mind it. The work had been good for him. Farm life had been a big change, but it gave him strength. Even Scotty was growing used to farm living. They now had three horses, and Shane was thinking of buying another.

"We need to head to the Dixon place! Now! Come on."

"What the hell is going on?"

"I saw it from the fields. Their mare, the brown speckled one, it's down."

"Not our business." Shane grumbled returning to the stall. He wouldn't consider himself a farmer, or horse trainer, but he was learning. He and Scotty fixed farm equipment for neighbors and the stipend from the government had been enough to buy their land. His mind was filled with ways to earn money honestly, and thoughts of Raelynn.

"Dammit Shane. I told you I wanted to get next to that blonde cutie, this is my chance. Come on!"

Shane sighed and tossed the shovel, then plucked off his gloves and tossed them as well. He looked around for his shirt.

"C'mon dammit!" Scotty yelled.

He had half a mind to kick his cousin's ass. He knew not to yell in the barn. Snatching up the shirt, he pulled it on then hurried out. Scotty was in his pickup. He had taken to wearing cowboy hats. Shane tried not to laugh. He was actually proud of his cousin's transformation. Besides a few bar fights and drunken nights, Scotty was his own man.

They drove out of the pasture and hit the road fast for the Dixon place. Shane loved the green richness of the land in Battle Creek. Still part of him couldn't quite call it home. Not that he ever had one. After he entered the Witness Protection Program all contact with his mother had ceased, and he felt no guilt over it. After what he learned about her and Cass, he couldn't summon sympathy. He did pray that she found peace wherever she was. Shane struggled more with the separation from Raelynn. He called her office several times to hear her voice on her voicemail. She didn't lose her job because of him. He took some pleasure in that. Once he called and she answered the phone, but he feared she'd put a trace on him, so he hung up. That was several months ago. He hadn't called again.

"Slow down Scotty." He warned.

They had different names now. Alone they'd slip into calling each other their true names. For Scotty he'd chosen Edward and Shane had settled on Tony. He had to keep reminding himself of his new identity in public.

Scotty drove to a stop right behind a blue pickup truck and nearly jumped out before putting it in park. All for some pretty blond he'd been salivating over for months. Shane got out of the pickup and sniffed his armpits. He didn't want to smell as bad as he looked, but it was unavoidable.

"Hi! Need help?" Scotty asked.

"Hi Edward," Susan said smiling. When her blue eyes fell over his way her smile spread even wider. "Hi Tony. Thanks for coming out here guys but you didn't have to. I already sent my brother Jake to call Doc Henry."

"What's wrong?" Shane asked.

Her smile dimmed and her gaze returned to the fallen mare. "She dropped, can't get her to stand. Not sure what caused it."

"Maybe she's pregnant?" Scotty gushed.

Shane shook his head and suppressed a smile. His cousin really was bad at this cowboy stuff. Susan chuckled as well. "No she's not pregnant, it's something else."

"Oh," said Scotty.

"Let's see." Shane walked over to the mare. He lowered and put a hand to her throat stroking softly. Susan and Scotty watched as he talked softly to the animal coaxing it to rise. A single pull of the reigns and the horse neighed, kicked its legs, and forced itself to stand. Even Shane was shocked over the feat.

"Well I'll be damn, you're a horse whisperer!" Scotty laughed.

Susan rushed the animal so excited. She flashed Shane a very sweet smile. "Thank you, how did you do that? What did you do?"

"I don't know. I just, I don't know."

"I owe you dinner." She smiled. "Tonight?"

Shane frowned. He looked back at his cousin and saw jealousy burning in Scotty's eyes. "How about Edward and I both come."

Susan smiled. "Okay. Thank you Tony. Thank you."

Two Weeks Later

"How's the Chief doing today?" Michael asked, holding the door for Raelynn to walk inside. She carried a dish of her macaroni in her hand. She promised to make him a pan and had some idle time on her hands. "He's better." She said going to the kitchen. "Doctors say he might come home next week."

"That soon huh?" Michael followed her into the kitchen.

"Yep. Man scared us to death. We will have to take better care of him." She set the dish in the oven and then closed the door.

"And?"

She turned to find Michael smiling at her again.

Raelynn smiled. "He knows. I couldn't hide it from him." She smoothed her hand down her small bulge.

"And?" Michael pressed.

Raelynn laughed. "He had questions, concerns, but you were right. He isn't angry with me for my mistakes. My baby isn't planned but it's not a mistake either. Daddy and I agree on that."

"See. I told you. The Chief is a good man."

"Yes, my father is." She nodded.

Since she'd been home they'd had dinner together four times, and spoke on the phone with each other every day. A habit was forming. She told him of Shane Lafferty, her mistakes, and their parting. She shared with him how much of a dead-end her job was before she left. She'd been passed over twice for an assignment. Her father woke to find her pregnant and unemployed at his bedside. She thought she'd disappoint and cause him stress and worry. But she should have known better. She should have come home sooner. All she found with her daddy was love and understanding.

Michael was indeed a friend. He listened about Shane. Even tried to convince her to use her contacts to locate him. Raelynn knew it would be a disaster if she did. Shane was free, finally. The last thing she wanted to do was drag him into her life after he discovered his own. "Why are you staring at me like that?"

"You need to stay Raelynn," he said, his voice serious.

"I brought the macaroni, of course I'll stay."

"You know what I mean. Don't go back to Boston. Not with the baby coming, stay here," he stepped toward her. Raelynn had to look away. A moment of weakness and she'd given this man too much information about her heart.

"It's complicated. I have to leave my life in Boston." She mumbled, and then reached to turn on the oven to avoid his questioning stare. She had planned to have the baby in Florida. She needed her parents. But she also needed a job, a career. Without law enforcement she felt lost.

Michael stopped her hand. He brought it to his lips. "I know you're not a quitter. I also know you're not happy in Boston. Raelynn, this is your home. Stay."

"You got it all figured out?" She laughed nervously. Michael's arm slipped around her waist. He brought her up against him. Her arms naturally circled his waist and her hands went to the defined planes of his back. He tilted her chin up with his finger. Her gaze lifted and locked with his. "Hey, I'm Sherriff in this town and I need a deputy. You yourself said you'd like to teach me a thing or two."

"What is it you're offering me?" Raelynn asked.

"What you need, a fresh start. Work with me. We could use your talents." Michael said, desire blazing in his eyes.

His body felt good pressed to hers. For a minute she could forget the loneliness she felt over losing Shane, but it was only brief. When he kissed her all she wanted was Shane. Michael must have felt it in her response. He pulled away. "I'm a patient man. I've cared about you for years Raelynn. Tell me you will think about it."

She sighed and rested her face against his chest. "I'll think about it."

***

"It's okay, it happens." Susan said, holding the sheet up to her breast.

Shane turned from her and zipped his pants. *It happens? Not to fucking him. Never to him!* "I think I should go."

"Tony! Wait."

Susan hurried from the bed. Shane sighed. He didn't want to hurt her, but he just couldn't get a reign on his emotions. The more his life changed, the more he missed and desired Raelynn. He only took Susan to bed to ease that ache, and to his surprise his body wouldn't respond.

"Don't go. Look at me. Look at me."

Shane turned his gaze to her. She touched his face. "I'm fine with it. I want you. I know you want me. We had a lot of beers tonight. Let's go slow okay?"

"I shouldn't be here. My cousin has a thing for you, this will crush him. Just forget about me okay." Shane headed for the door. He stopped himself and looked back at Susan who stood there dejected and hurt. "I'm sorry babe. It's not you. Hell yes, I want you. Any man would. I'm just too screwed up now. You understand?"

"No." She said sadly.

"Yeah, me either."

EPILOGUE

One Year Later

"Got a call." Michael walked in. Raelynn looked up from behind her desk. She'd just got in from patrols and had hoped she'd see him.

"What call?"

"The horse trade shows, down off Simon Road. Traffic is a monster, we need all extra hands. Can you get out there and make sure the locals don't get too out of hand."

Raelynn smiled. She rose from her desk. "So now I'm a traffic cop?"

"The sexiest traffic cop I've ever seen." He winked.

"Careful Sherriff, you might get hit with a sexual harassment suit." Raelynn chuckled. She caught the look of longing in his eyes. She tried to ignore it. She and Michael were better off as friends. In fact he had been the best friend she needed. He helped her move and settle back into their small town. He had been there through the birth of her son. And now he'd given her a job that fulfilled her. They tried to pursue more but Raelynn could never give him her heart. He said he understood and could be patient. Raelynn knew better. Every time she looked at her little boy she thought of Shane. She even called Andy and tried to get information on where he was. But Andy couldn't access Shane's file. Once a candidate went in the WPP few people in the bureau had access to their information. So she decided love wouldn't be an option for her, motherhood would suffice. Michael dated Debbie Scalar now, and that viper would claw her eyes out if she caught the looks he gave her.

She put on her deputy hat and picked up her gun holster. "I'll check it out. Make sure everything is okay."

"Radio in if you need assistance."

Raelynn winked at him and walked out. She couldn't be happier. Life in her small town went on pleasantly for the most part. They had their crime, gangs, robberies, and even a few murders. But for the most part she could breathe again. Andrea and Olivia had traveled in to see her baby boy. They made plans to get together again during the summer. The regret and sadness she had for Shane Lafferty had healed. She was Deputy Raelynn Traylor now, and happy.

The drive to Simon Road had only been manageable when she hit her police lights. The cars moved out of her path or hurried along clearing the way. She saw a few of their officers on duty and signaled to them that she would park and join them. She found a spot near some parked trailers. The Annual Ruffington Horse Trade Convention had been going on for two days, and would extend into the weekend. There would be parties, even a rodeo out on Ruffington Farm, which meant a lot of drinking and stupid disorderly behavior. She doubted she'd have any time for her baby over the weekend because of it.

Raelynn walked through the tall grass through the trailers and toward the tents. The speaker box on her shoulder announced a crowd control unit to the north of the convention. She figured the trade shows would start soon. Her presence sometimes calmed the locals and made them behave a bit better than usual. Continuing her trek, she saw a man in Wranglers and a Stetson locking down the back of a trailer. His body looked fit, he wore a white-striped shirt rolled up at the sleeve. The tattoo on his forearm gave her pause. A gothic cross she'd know anywhere. His head turned at someone calling the name 'Tony'. Raelynn froze. The shamrock tattooed on his neck came into view. And though the bib of the Stetson was pulled down low over his eyes and covered the top part of his face, she'd know him anywhere.

"Shane?"

A petite blonde walked over with a baby in her arms, and handed him a bottle of water. He leaned over and kissed her cheek. Raelynn felt her chest cave in at the scene. *Shane with a woman, a baby, his family?* Panic seized her limbs making her retreat stiff and awkward. Raelynn turned and hurried toward a crowd to slip through. She could barely catch her breath. Was it him? It had to be him? Did he move on? Yes! Yes! He moved on.

"Oh God help me. He moved on." She panted.

"Where's your husband?" Shane asked Susan.

"He couldn't wait to get into the trade show, left me and his son behind." Susan frowned. The baby gave Shane a wide toothless grin.

"Hand me my little cousin. You go after him. Have some fun."

"No Shane, you've been working hard all day. Little Eddie is a handful. I'll put him to sleep in the trailer."

"Nonsense." Shane took the two month old out of her hands. The baby nearly disappeared in the crook of his arm. He smiled at his baby cousin whose eyes closed immediately. "See, the kid likes me."

"Okay Uncle Tony, I will be back. Just want to find that man of mine and make sure he doesn't sell our entire farm for a damn colt."

Shane laughed. He watched Susan run off. The past year had been a huge change for him and his cousin. Scotty and Susan's courtship was brief before she turned up pregnant. In Battle Creek an unexpected pregnancy presented a man with two options: marriage or a shotgun blast to the chest. So Scotty stood in front of a local preacher and said his 'I dos'. To Shane's surprise it transformed Scotty into Edward. His cousin thrived in his new life as a husband, farmer, and dad. He couldn't be more proud of him.

Shane walked away from the trailer balancing the baby in the crook of his arm. He felt restless, didn't want to sit with the kid. The crowds had thinned and headed to the trade show, so his stroll down toward the tents was unobstructed. He stopped and looked at a booth of saddles, a few leather wares, and then some custom belt buckles that reminded him of the heavyweight title belt he passed on by leaving his boxing career behind. Feeling the night air get a bit choppy he turned to head back and saw her.

Or he thought he did.

A black woman in a deputy's hat walked out from under a tent and met his stare. There were a few times over the past year when he thought he saw Raelynn, and all of them had been his imagination. This time the resemblance stopped him cold. She turned and immediately started to walk away.

"Rae? Rae!" he shouted and the baby began to cry. Shane rocked him in his arms and hurried after her. "Rae!"

Finally she stopped. She removed her hat and turned to face him. *It was her.* His Raelynn. Shane stared at her in disbelief. He just stood there in shock.

"Hi Shane."

"You saw me, didn't you? You were going to walk away?"

Raelynn's gaze shifted to the baby, but Shane couldn't take his eyes off of her. He wanted to touch her. Hell he wanted to grab her and kiss her. How long had he dreamed of this moment? Prayed for it?

"What's your son's name?"

The question hit him like a lightening bolt. He snapped out of his fog and realized his cousin sucked hard on his pacifier, staring directly at Raelynn. "He's um, he's not my son… he's my cousin. Scotty's son."

Raelynn seemed surprised. "Oh," she then forced a smile. "Strange coincidence huh? Seeing each other."

Shane frowned at her deputy uniform. He knew she was at the FBI so was she undercover or something? Raelynn must have sensed his question. She laughed. "I'm from Pensacola. I um, came back home. I work for the Sherriff's office now."

"You do?"

"I do." Raelynn smiled. "It was good seeing you again Shane. Take care." She put her hat back on and turned to walk away.

"Don't do it Rae," he said. She stopped. "Don't walk away from me again. It's been over a year, and I still can't stand it when you walk away."

She looked back at him, her eyes glistening with an apology. "I never wanted to walk away from you Shane. I had no choice."

"And now? Do you have a choice?"

"Who's the blonde?" She asked.

Shane frowned. "The what?"

"I saw you with your, um, wife?" Raelynn said.

Shane smiled. "She's Scotty's wife, and this is their kid. Rae, there is so much I need to say to you. Please."

She pressed her lips together. Taking in a deep breath, she reached in her pocket and withdrew her wallet. She pulled out a card, then unclipped the pin tucked inside her front uniform pocket. She scribbled something and passed him the card. "I guess you're a cowboy now huh?" She said with a weak smile. "I owe you an explanation, I owe you so much Shane."

"Owe me? I don't understand?" Shane frowned.

"Here's my address, I get off at eleven."

Shane accepted the card. Raelynn touched the hand of the baby and cooed at him. She looked up at him again and so much desire passed between them in that brief exchange. Shane forgot to breathe. He nodded that he'd call her and she walked away.

Raelynn forced her legs to remain steady. She was grateful for the wind; it dried the tears streaming down her cheeks. How could she possibly face him now? Tell him about their son, and the missed opportunities he was denied. Would he hate her? Blame her? Her heart raced so bad she could barely manage it. After she'd walked far enough away she looked back to see him still staring after her. Her heart turned over. She felt the flutter of a hundred butterflies in the pit of her stomach. He'd changed. So had she. Who were they now?

**

Shane turned off his headlights. Raelynn's house was a small box shaped cottage. Not as fancy as the brownstone she had in Boston. He saw a blue Chevy parked in the drive and the front porch light was on. He didn't tell Scotty about seeing her. He wasn't sure why. At that moment he just wanted them again, and didn't feel the need to explain or justify it. He sat there for several minutes staring at her house, wondering about her life. A year was a long time. What if she didn't feel the way he did? What if she still regretted their time together? He had so many damn 'what ifs'.

Releasing a deep sigh, he threw open the car door to face it. Either way he needed this reunion just to move on. He was stuck in limbo because of his feelings for her. He wanted to tell her his heart and make her understand how grateful he was for her saving his life, for believing in him. Then maybe he'd be able to let her go.

Shane left the car. Raelynn stepped back from the blinds. She'd watched him since he drove up. Her mother, who had become her on-call babysitter, had left an hour ago. She called Andrea and told her that she saw Shane and he would be coming to meet his son.

Andrea laughed, saying she did her horoscope and her moon was in Venus, a sign for new love. Raelynn believed it. Damn it she wanted to believe it. He looked so handsome. The cowboy hat he wore instead of a baseball cap aged him. He looked settled, like a man, not a victim or a thug. Raelynn hurried to the door and stopped in front of it. She fixed her shirt and looked down at her jean skirt she'd chosen to wear. It made her legs look nice. But she had curves now, a pudgy stomach she couldn't shed and stretch marks too around her hips. Maybe she should have put on jeans.

The doorbell rang.

Raelynn's breath caught in her throat. She sucked down deep breaths of air and tried to calm herself. She didn't want her son to wake and accelerate the reunion. She had to do this right.

The doorbell rang again.

"Shit!"

Raelynn opened the door and smiled. Shane smiled.

"Hi"

"Hi," he said.

"Oh, come in." She stepped back and let him walk through the door. His cologne drifted under her nose as he passed. She inhaled deeply. "I know it's late. Thanks for coming."

"You alone?" Shane asked looking around.

"I live alone. I'm a big girl remember? I can take care of myself."

Shane cut her a look from over his shoulder. He removed his hat. She immediately wanted to touch his hair that lay finely on his brow and extended to his sideburns. He had a light mustache but other than that, it was him. All him.

"Can I get you something to drink?" Raelynn asked.

"Sure."

Raelynn hurried past him. She went into the kitchen and got two beers. She walked out to find him seated on her sofa. Raelynn turned on the lamp to cast more light into the room. She handed him a beer. "Wow. Weird we'd see each other this way. Huh?"

Shane just stared at her. He sipped his beer.

Raelynn downed a big swallow to wash out her nerves. She licked her lips. "Shane, I…"

"Why did you leave the FBI?" he asked.

Her heart skipped a beat. "It's a long story."

"I gather that, but I feel like it was something more. Was it because of us?"

Raelynn pressed her lips together trying to decide if she could speak truthfully to him. If he was involved with someone and just there for closure, she needed to be careful of the wounds she cut open. Telling him about his son should be her only priority. "I, um, there's something you need to know."

"Rae. It's been a long time. I know I have no right to come here and question you. I've missed you. There I said it. I just want to know, I need to know if it was all in my head."

"If what was all in your head?" Raelynn asked.

"Us, what we felt, what we were that short time together. You kept saying it would end. For me, it never did."

Raelynn didn't know what to say. She blinked at him, confused. Was he actually saying he cared, even now? "We only knew each other for a week."

"And I've spent over a year trying to forget that week. I haven't. Have you?"

Raelynn smiled. "No. I couldn't." She rose. She walked over to the bookshelf and picked up a picture concealed by the shadows of her home. When she turned to see him watching, waiting she nearly lost her nerve. "His name is Shawn."

"Who?" Shane asked. "You're boyfriend? Husband?"

Raelynn sniffed. She exhaled slowly. Shane's gaze dropped from her face to the picture frame. Raelynn stepped closer and handed it to him. "Your son."

Shane accepted the photo. He stared at the image expressionless. It went on for an eternity, his silent stare, before his gaze slowly lifted.

"My son?"

"A month into your trial I found out I was pregnant. I couldn't believe it Shane. We were careful. We used protection every time, but I was pregnant."

"My son?" he repeated.

"Listen to me. I wanted to tell you. But you were in custody, and I had no access to you. My job was on the line, my life too. I didn't know what to do. I took leave from the FBI then I just resigned. And by then you were gone. My dad took sick and…" Raelynn closed her eyes. "There is no excuse. You should have been told." She opened her eyes. "Forgive me."

Shane stared at the image.

"Do you want to meet him?"

"He's here?"

She nodded. "He's seven months. He looks so much like you." She extended her hand. Shane didn't reach for it. He stared up at her with sadness, anger, disappointment, shock in his eyes. She knew he couldn't decide on which emotion to hold on to.

"You were pregnant and you didn't tell me?"

"Shane…"

"Stop it Rae! You kept him from me because you didn't want me in his life. You saw me at the trade show and you walked away. Dammit how could you do that?"

Raelynn swallowed the sob in her throat. "I panicked. I saw you and I panicked. You had a baby in your arms and a woman. You have a life Shane. Finally you have your own life. I couldn't walk up to you and take it away."

"Bullshit! You ran from me because it was easier for you. You never wanted anything with me, not even our kid!"

"Don't you dare say that to me!" Raelynn wiped the loose tear from her cheek. "I love my baby and I never considered him a mistake, never! You can get the hell out of you think he is."

Shane let go a deep breath. "This is my fault. I ruined your life."

"No."

"Yes." Shane nodded his head. "The night we made love at your friend's house, we didn't use a condom. I should have told you. I didn't plan it, but it happened. I thought you'd blame me or something so I didn't say anything."

Raelynn blinked at him shocked. "Why would you keep that

from me?"

"Same reason you kept my son from me. Fear Rae. Insecurity, hell selfishness, neither of us are without blame." He rose. Raelynn stepped back. Her chest grew tight with anger. She felt dizzy from the crushing wave of emotions going through her. Shane grabbed her arms. "I'm sorry, but I want to see my boy now. Please."

Raelynn couldn't speak. She just nodded and stepped away. She led him to Shawn's room. The light from the moon fell over his crib. Their baby slept under his blanket with his pacifier in his mouth. His hands were balled into tight fists. "Can I hold him? I'll be careful."

"He's sleep. But, um, okay." She reached in the crib but Shane lifted him into his arms. To see him hold their baby shook her to her core. She forgot the reasons for her anger and disappointment. She actually felt relief. Shane smiled at Shawn who squirmed and sucked harder on his pacifier. He weighed a ton with his chubby arms and legs, but Shane held him without effort.

"He looks like you Rae."

"Wait until he opens his eyes. He looks like you Shane." Raelynn said.

"I love him." Shane announced. He looked up at her and nodded. "I love him, and I love you Rae. I don't care if you don't believe me. I can't explain to you why, but it's true. I love you."

Raelynn opened her mouth to say the same and hesitated, then found the strength in her vocal chords to speak. "I left the FBI because I couldn't forget Shane. I came home and I tried to forget, even tried to start another... um, tried to start over. I didn't, um, couldn't. Not just because of the baby. It was you, what we shared. I didn't understand how much I cared about you until you were gone. Forgive me for not telling you about Shawn. Forgive me for not trying harder to find you."

Shane carefully placed their child in the crib. He took her into his arms and held her before he walked her back out to the sofa. Raelynn took a moment to catch her breath. Her heart raced and pounded in her chest. Seated next to him she still struggled to speak, but she needed to tell him all the things she never did. She set her clammy palms over her lap. "There is so much we need to talk about. So much I want to know about you now Shane."

"Name's Tony." He smirked.

Raelynn laughed. "Tony. I want to know more about you."

"Come closer, and I'll tell you."

Raelynn moved in closer. Shane stretched his arm over the top of the sofa so she could fit nicely. She did. The moment she turned her face to speak, his lips brushed hers, and soon his tongue delved deeply. It was the spark that ignited the flames of desire she had buried deep within. Raelynn moved in on him, returning his kiss. Shane moved her to his lap and Raelynn parted her thighs to straddle him, her jean skirt pushed up to her hips and she situated herself over his bulge. His body trembled beneath her; she felt his building desire about to push him into overload. She grabbed his face and controlled their passion. Raelynn felt him fiddling with his belt and zipper. She pushed up on her knees, her tongue swirling around his, their barley laced breaths mingling.

And without thought of caution, responding on pure instinct, he pushed her panty aside and thrust his cock up into her. Raelynn bit down on his bottom lip, the upward thrust came too fast and swift, stretching her unmercifully. Shane didn't flinch.

Shane's hands gripped her thighs and he drove her up and down on his shaft until he filled her completely. She moved for him, working him over with her hip rotation. Shane groaned and she hid her face against his shoulder to conceal the pure joy rippling through her. Her inner walls clenched and convulsed around his upward jerking cock. She held on to him until she exploded.

"I'm not done with you yet Rae, not by a long shot." He lifted her gently from his still angrily erect cock. Raelynn weakly fell over to the sofa. "Where is the bedroom?"

"There…" she panted and pointed. Shane rose. He stood over her. Raelynn closed her thighs realizing how crudely she was posed. He smiled. "You know once I take you into that bedroom, make love you to truly, I'm never leaving you again," he said.

"We have to talk, our lives, who we are… the program. Shawn, he's my priority Shane."

"We'll figure it out. As long as you promise me that you'll be mine again, you and Shawn."

Raelynn stared up at him, his penis thick and swollen outside of his jean zipper, and his face tight with desire, and pain. She knew what he needed. God help her she needed it too. Raelynn sat up and she smiled. "I'll never let you go baby." She took hold of his cock and guided it over her tongue, swallowing several inches.

Shane groaned. His hand cupped the back of her head as he instructed her on how to love him. Raelynn sucked harder, working her fist around the base of his shaft, and rolling her tongue over his thickness. Soon he was pushing her away and pulling her up into his arms. She slipped him her tongue once more, tasting and smelling of him. He kissed her deeply. Then he released her.

"I never told you." He panted.

"Told me what?" Raelynn said, licking her lips, thinking of the loneliness that would finally be replaced with him. The life they could have, truly believing in second chances.

"I forgive you," he said.

"Shane Lafferty, I forgive you too."

"Show me." he kissed her. Shane swept her into his arms and carried her out of the living room to the bedroom. She held tightly to him. Today would be the first day of the rest of their lives.

ABOUT THE AUTHOR

Sienna Mynx is your naughty writer of Paranormal, Contemporary, and Historical Interracial Romance for readers who love the bad boys but desire to be the woman who tames them. Sienna Mynx's novellas reflect her thirst for romance, told from a fresh perspective with the diversity she craves in erotic romance.

A current resident of south Georgia, Sienna Mynx is currently at work on a military-themed romance, a paranormal anthology, and the sequels to her bestsellers "Daisy's Choice" and "St. Patty's Baby!" Look for more to come. Visit Sienna Mynx at http://thedivaspen.com.

Made in the USA
Charleston, SC
29 March 2012